JOHN BATHGATE

INHERENT
EVIL

And He Walked in All the Sins
His Father Did Before Him
(1Kings 15:3)

authorHOUSE

AuthorHouse™ UK
1663 Liberty Drive
Bloomington, IN 47403 USA
www.authorhouse.co.uk
Phone: 0800.197.4150

Published by AuthorHouse 06/28/2017

ISBN: 978-1-5246-8257-6 (sc)
ISBN: 978-1-5246-8256-9 (e)

PROLOGUE

Mary lay on the pavement where her attacker had left her, barely conscious, unable to move her arms and legs and prevented from calling out by the tape around her mouth. When a passing neighbour, returning from the city centre celebrations with her daughter, stopped to help, she hardly recognized the girl she had known for several years. They removed the tape from her mouth and the bindings from her hands and feet, then led Mary home. Mary gave no indication of even recognising her mother who was shocked to see the state her daughter was in. Her mother ran to the phone-box at the end of their street and made an emergency 999 call for an ambulance. She then left a message for her husband at the car-factory where he was on night shift.

On such a night of revelry, with the raised level of alcohol consumption in the city, Coventry City Hospital was stretched to the limit, and it was almost an hour before the ambulance arrived at the house. By then Mary appeared to have relapsed into a comatose state. She couldn't answer the questions her father asked, and made no coherent sounds at all.

On arrival at the hospital a woman doctor examined Mary closely, and called for the police to attend as it was clear that there had been serious sexual assault as well as the blows she had sustained to her head. It was nearly dawn when a police sergeant and a young constable arrived on the scene. By then the doctor had been able to confirm the extent of Mary's injuries. Without any statement from the victim, and with no apparent witnesses to how or where the rape had taken place, the police were completely in the dark. Mary was shown photographs of potential suspects, but she showed no sign of recognition. Despite appeals to the public, none of which gave any indication of the victim's name, there was no response.

Mary remained in a comatose state for several weeks, initially in hospital, and later at home. Although physically she appeared to be unharmed, able to be out of bed to attend to her own physical functions, and to eat normally, Mary seemed like a zombie, with no interest in anything that happened around her. This situation continued even after it was discovered that she was pregnant.

CHAPTER 1

On a dull Sunday morning in October 1973 in the garrison town of Aldershot. Sergeant Tom Mitchell was contemplating the bleak outlook from the window of his Military Police office, looking forward to his demobilization in just two weeks, when he would be returning to his native town, Edinburgh. He had just made himself his first cup of coffee of the day and settled himself at the desk when his phone rang.

The caller introduced himself as the adjutant at a local Ordnance Corps barracks. "Sergeant Mitchell, my Regimental Sergeant Major has informed me of an incident that took place involving some of our lads last night. I've not got the full details yet, but there is a soldier lying in bed in Cambridge Military Hospital rather badly injured. Could you come out here to talk to my RSM and look into it? Oh, and we're due a visit from a local Police Inspector later on. Apparently one of the civilians who were involved in the incident was found dead in a local park this morning. You should be there to talk to him."

1

Tom Mitchell heaved a big sigh. This close to demob he didn't want to get involved in some case that was likely to run on, so he tried to put the adjutant off by suggesting that he should initiate the inquiry himself if it only involved his own men.

"Oh, I'm sorry" said the adjutant. I should have made myself clearer. The soldiers involved aren't my men. They are part of a group who are assembling to attend a fire-fighting course with us. The soldier who is in hospital is a paratrooper who arrived just yesterday. There was some kind of to-do involving some civilians. I think you should get out here as fast as you can. Tom finished his coffee then made his way to the Ordnance Corps barracks where he was met by RSM Clark. The RSM, a mountain of a man, towered about three inches above Tom's six- eet two, and outweighed him by about three stones, making Tom feel distinctly puny. Obviously upset at having to forego his Sunday break, the RSM immediately went straight into his explanation of what had happened.

"We had four chaps come in yesterday for a fire-fighting course that is to start tomorrow. There are to be twenty of them, all from different regiments. The rest will arrive today. Apparently the four of them went out for a drink last night. I'm told there was a bit of an argument between them and a gang of civilians in a local pub, the only one that our own chaps don't use. There has been trouble there in the past. They tell me that nothing came of the argument, no fisticuffs or anything, but on their way back to camp one of them got separated from the others. They heard some noises and went back for him. He was lying in the street with a badly cut hand, and some serious injuries to his face.

He`s not been able to talk so we don`t know the whys and wherefores of it."

Tom immediately asked to see the other soldiers who had been with the injured man. When they arrived they all appeared hung over. Before going into the individual statements that he would require from each of them, he asked where they had picked up their injured companion so that he could check on any available evidence. Luckily they had only been a few hundred yards from the camp when they had heard the breaking of glass and the loud scream of pain that had made them retrace their steps.

The three soldiers accompanied Tom along the narrow road that led to the barracks, eventually stopping where they could see blood stains on the pavement. As well as the bloodstains there was a considerable amount of broken glass which Tom carefully photographed with his Polaroid camera. Tom noticed there were some drops of blood trailing back from the large stain. He traced the spots back some fifty yards or more then found another large stain. It seemed clear that the two injuries the paratrooper had suffered, to his hand and to his face, were in fact the result of more than one scuffle. Tom took two samples of blood, one from each of the large stains, thinking that it was fortunate that there had not been heavy rain during the night.

He questioned the three soldiers one by one and got similar stories from all of them. He later summarised their statements as follows.

All four had arrived at the barracks, separately, the previous afternoon. With the others on the course they would occupy a single barrack block. The course was for junior NCO`s only. When it was apparent that none of the others would arrive that evening, they decided to go into the nearby town of Cove for a drink. Still dressed in uniform, they booked out at the guardhouse and walked into Cove, a distance of less than a mile. They selected a pub where there seemed to be a lot of unaccompanied young women, and which was blaring out popular music. As they entered they removed their berets and placed them inside their battledress blouses.

Their presence seemed to attract a lot of attention. This struck them as strange, but they sat down at a table and ordered drinks. The barman suggested they try his famous scrumpy cider, which none of them had ever tried before. Three of them tried it, but the fourth ordered a soft drink. Before long a group of young women entered the pub and accepted an invitation to join the soldiers.

There was obviously a lot of unrest among the local men who were in the pub when the women pulled a table up to join the soldiers, and they quickly paired up. One of the women explained that it was always the same when they sat with soldiers from the local camp. The locals got angry and tried to start an argument. None of the four wanted to start any trouble so they did not respond when some youths started to express their opinions about them. The landlord shouted out above the music and the voices of the youths to have some order, and the place settled down.

The four couples automatically paired off and conversations started, but as the drinks started to take effect, there were some close embraces exchanged, except by the coke drinker and the girl beside him. He was the one who finished up injured, she was the youngest and prettiest of the women. They both seemed reticent about carrying on as the other three couples were, and appeared to have started a scrappy conversation.

The three scrumpy drinkers stayed with their chose drinks as the evening's drinking progressed, the entire atmosphere within the pub became more unruly. People started to sing to the popular songs that were being played, but a group of noisy youths started to shout out comments about the morals of girls who drank with soldiers, and about the nerve of the soldiers in monopolizing the group of women.

The landlord kept calling for order, but the catcalls became more and more inflammatory. It looked as if the situation would become violent when the sober soldier, Lance Corporal Jim Doyle called to the youths to keep quiet. His exact words were

"Why don't you English bastards keep yer fucking mouths shut?" The coarse Glasgow accent provoked silence for a few seconds, but then pandemonium broke out. Not only did the youths start back at him, but most of the local males joined in.

One youth, bigger than all the others, and just as drunk, rushed forward to face up to the Scotsman. Doyle stood up to him, showing no sign of fear. The landlord came from behind the bar to keep the two apart, but the youth in particular was prepared to do battle. "You Scotch bastard" he screamed, obviously incensed, "come out the back. I'll fucking kill you."

Doyle remained quite calm "oh, just go and sit down. Let us all enjoy our drinks."

His calmness irritated the young man even more and he tried to push the landlord aside to get at him. At that, the landlord and one of the barmen took him by the arms and ushered him out of the bar, with a warning not to come back. He then asked Doyle and his mates to leave.

They went peacefully, albeit reluctantly on the part of Doyle's three mates, all of whom had fancied their chances of having it off with the girls they had been paired up with. When they got outside they started at him about spoiling their chances but he mocked them by telling them that after several pints of scrumpy they had no chance of managing sex that night anyway.

They started to walk down the road that would take them to the camp. As they passed a fish and chip shop Doyle announced that he was going to get some chips and that he would catch up on them. The three walked on, soon turning the corner at the end of the road so that Doyle was out of sight.

Slowed down by the amount of cider they had drunk, they had not travelled very far when they heard some shouts from behind them, followed by a piercing scream. They ran back towards the town, turned the corner and saw Doyle staggering towards them, and three figures disappearing further up the road. Doyle's right hand had a bloody handkerchief around it and his face looked as if it had been through a mangle, his mouth extended and his nosed knocked to one side. They took him back to the camp where the guard commander phoned for an ambulance.

The three soldiers were then bundled off to bed, much the worse for wear, and warned that they would have to see the RSM in the morning.

The RSM confirmed to Tom that he had heard their story earlier that morning, and had reported to the adjutant.

No one had yet told the civil police about the incident. As the RSM commented,

"we thought it better to talk to you first. I thought you might prefer to keep it away from the police. Can we not deal with this ourselves?"

Tom was non-commital. "I'll wait until I've spoken to this chap Doyle before I make up my mind about that." But the decision was taken out of his hands.

As he prepared to drive into Aldershot to see Lance Corporal Doyle in Cambridge Military Hospital a police car drew into the barracks. The plain clothed man who came into the guardroom recognised the Military Police uniform that Tom Mitchell was wearing and addressed him. "God, you're here quick. Are you going to tell me that your chaps are already under arrest?

"Under arrest? What for? One of them is so badly hurt that he is lying in hospital."

The police inspector paused. "Are we talking about the same thing? I'm looking for the person responsible for the murder of a young man from Cove. Earlier, he was facing up to one of your men, ready to fight him. He was found dead this morning in the local park.",

"I think you are looking in the wrong place", said Tom, nobody here was involved in any murder. In fact, I was going to come to you to see if you knew who had been responsible for the assault on one of our chaps."

At that the inspector suggested that they should sit down somewhere and discuss the situation. Tom, the inspector, a detective sergeant and the RSM went into a room at the back of the guardroom and settled down to hear the respective stories. Tom spoke of the statements that he had from the three soldiers and stated that none of them had been in any state to do anything other than come straight back to camp after leaving the pub. The inspector listened to what Tom had told him with a look of incredulity on his face, and suggested that the statements had been a pack of lies. That morning he had already spoken to the landlord of the pub where they had been drinking. His story was virtually the same as the soldiers, up to the point where they had been ejected. However, he had also stated that the angry youth's friends had also left the pub shortly after the soldiers.

The police had been informed around daybreak that a body had been found in the park. The informant was the dead man's brother. His story was that they had all gone looking for their friend in the other pubs in the town. When they could not find him at any of their usual haunts, they all went home. The informant had had a restless night listening for the return of his brother. At dawn he had left the house to look for him again, and found his body in the park. He had immediately called the police. The brother confirmed that the dead man had been involved in an argument with one of the soldiers in the pub. This had led to the inspector interviewing the landlord of the pub, hence his interest in talking to the soldiers who had been in the pub the previous night.

The cause of death had not yet been established, but an autopsy was due to be held as soon as possible.

The story did not seem very convincing to Tom who had been impressed by the convincing statements that the three unhurt soldiers had made including their having seen some men running away from where Doyle had been hurt. Tom Mitchell poo- poohed the story then took the inspector and his sergeant to see the blood where Doyle had been assaulted. He then left them to carry out their own investigations and made his way to the hospital to get a statement from the Lance Corporal.

On his arrival at the hospital Tom was informed that Doyle was still heavily sedated. The surgeon had operated on his injuries in the late morning and wouldn't permit any questioning about the incident until the following morning. When he asked whether Doyle was in a secure ward, he was assured that he would be in no state to move for the next twenty-four hours at least, so Tom left after arranging to visit the following morning.

As he drove back to his office Tom pondered the situation. He had been involved with the civilian police on major cases before. Usually he had managed to contrive a position where they had agreed that the army and the civil police would deal with their own people. However, he had never had a soldier accused of murder. He had a sinking feeling that these last couple of weeks before his demob were going to be a lot busier that he had been looking forward to. The involvement with the police this time was likely to be extensive, and he couldn't see a way to keep things separate.

When he wrote his report on the case he wryly thought that this was going to be the biggest case of his life. As usual it was going to be a case of conflict between Army and civilian police. How on earth was it going to turn out?

Chapter 2

Doyle opened his eyes with a struggle. His whole head felt heavy and bloated and the area around his nose was painful. The surroundings were unfamiliar to him, reminding him of a tent, but there was no recollection of camping or travelling to get into such a situation. The veil that had seemed to him to be the tent sides gradually became focused and he realized that he was protected from the immediate world around him by screens that could only be the type that provided some kind of privacy in a hospital ward. This was not because he had had any first-hand experience of hospitals, but some of the popular hospital movies he had seen had started off with just the kind of situation that he now appeared to be starring in.

There was no immediate recall of how or why he should find himself in this situation and he didn't feel capable of working it out for himself. The place was bright enough, everything sterile white, apart from the shiny metal rail that was just a few inches from his eyes when he turned them to left or right. His position in the bed seemed unnatural. He couldn't remember ever having wakened in such a position in his life. He was flat on his back, sheets and blankets up to his armpits, with his left arm under the sheet and the right one lying by his side, on top of the blanket. As he became more aware of his surroundings he realised that there was a dull pain in his right hand and when he raised it from the elbow he could see that it was bound by a heavy bandage. Without moving his head, which felt as if it belonged on the shoulders of some large furry animal with an extended snout, he freed his left hand from the sheet to try and discover what was wrong with his face and head.

He felt so groggy that this simple movement sent tremors through his body. Just as his hand was rising, he heard the curtains being drawn aside and a female voice, with a soft Irish accent said, `You don`t want to be moving yet, just lie still` He made no further effort to raise his hand, just letting it fall back on the blankets. He tried to ask where he was, but couldn`t get the words out of his mouth which now started to send spasms of pain screaming into his brain. So many thoughts came into his mind that he felt scared. What had they done to him? Was this how he was to spend the rest of his life? How on earth had all this happened?

The nurse, she had to be a nurse, or was this heaven, and was this an angel come to prepare him for his new life? But the voice came back again. "You are still groggy after your operation. We thought it would take longer before you came round." Again he couldn`t articulate any words. His mouth was covered over and no sounds could be made.

"Don`t try and talk now, I`ll give you another sedative and when you waken I`ll get the surgeon to talk to you."

It was several hours later when Jim woke again. This time he felt less panicky than he had done previously, but still tried to find out what was wrong with his face. He tried to run his tongue round his mouth, but didn't get very far. He couldn't get his tongue between his lips, which seemed to be fixed together, although he was aware of a slight gap on the left side. His tongue located several sharp spiky things which he gradually came to accept as being stitches, but where his two front teeth should have been there was an ominous gap. He was reluctant to lift his right hand which was heavily bandaged, but he tentatively raised his left to play around the area of his mouth.

He could feel what seemed like an adhesive bandage that stretched from the left side of his mouth to the jawbone on the right, from the top of his nose to just above his chin. One small gap at the left of his mouth appeared to have been left to allow him to breathe. Little wonder that he had not been able to speak, or that he could not put his tongue past his lips, but why had they had to pull his front two teeth?

As he was considering these things, the curtain opened again and the same nurse stood at his side, looking even more like an angel, now that his mind had cleared enough to appreciate the dark good looks of the girl. "Good" she said, "you look a lot more awake now than you did before. I'm sorry I had to put you back to sleep. I'll get the doctor to come and see you."

When the doctor arrived, he introduced himself and said, "I am glad to see you awake, we were very worried about you for a while." Jim tried to speak, but the small opening left for breathing did not permit any coherent words to come through, so he pointed to his mouth and shook his head.

The doctor appreciated the situation and told Jim, "It will be a few days before we can take away those bandages, so you had better get used to just listening for a while. I know it must seem drastic to you but we are very hopeful that you will get the full use of everything again. When we first saw you we feared that you might be terribly disfigured, but things went well once we found the real extent of your injuries. Your hand is likely to cause you the most trouble for the tendons have been severed and will take some time to heal."

"Do you know anything about what happened to you? No, that's stupid of me. I'll tell you what I know. The ambulance driver who brought you here wasn't able to tell us much, but it seems that you were attacked by several chaps in a dark street. When we saw you, it was clear you had been struck very heavily on the face, because your nose was almost lifted away and it looked as if you had a broken jaw or cheek bone on the right. Our surgeon wasn't available when you arrived but we weren't worried, the bones are easily set for some time after an accident. It was only after we x-rayed your face that we discovered that there was no broken bones, but the swelling on your face was in fact a piece of glass embedded in your cheek. When we found that we had to operate quickly to prevent any complications. You might be interested in this."

He picked up a small porcelain container from a bedside cupboard and showed Jim a lump of glass about the size of a half-crown. The glass was thick and looked to be from the lower part of a beer glass. "That must have been a hell of a blow to break glass that thick. Once we got rid of that it was just a case of getting things put back into the right places- except for your teeth. The front two broke off at the gum. Apart from your hand this will cause you the most trouble, but we can`t do anything until your mouth is completely healed. Really, you are a lucky young man that the blow didn`t kill you. Just a little bit higher and there`s no telling what kind of damage might have occurred. It`s just as well you are a big chap. However, I expect you to be up and about within a few days, but you will be with us for quite a while. I`ll see you again tomorrow morning."

The doctor left, then the nurse straightened up his bed, and said to Jim, "you won`t be able to eat anything solid for a while, but I can give you something through a straw. They thought about that when they sewed you up and left a little gap in the dressings.

Would you like something now?" Jim shook his head and settled back into the pillows.

There was no prospect of sleeping for some time, but Jim now had time to think. Vague memories of the previous night came back to him, but after the slashing blow on his hand he could remember very little. He peered at the bandaged hand, but nothing could be seen, and it was too tightly bound to be able to try and wiggle his fingers, but as he tried to recall the blow, it came back to him that he had actually completed the complicated manoeuvre that he had been practising at Karate for many years. That swing to the right with his hand and forearm had been completely intuitive, and having started the move he had also gone into the follow up by pirouetting to his left, delivering a rabbit punch towards the throat and then kicking at his opponent`s groin.

He had experienced some satisfaction on the completion of the move, for he knew that it had been done to perfection

But had he stopped short of actually hitting his attacker as he had done in a thousand practices? Or had he gone through with a potentially lethal move He seemed to remember the blows actually landing and seeing the chap on the ground before he ran off, but nobody had said anything about anyone else being injured.

He then recalled seeing the blood spurting from his hand, and stopping to try and stem the bleeding with his handkerchief. That was when the world had exploded. His head seemed to pop and then he had run away from whoever had hit him. That thought worried him. After all those years of training he had run away when he was struck? He must have known instinctively that he was out of the fight after that blow. But he was no coward. He remembered his younger days before he started to attend Karate lessons. At that time he was a real bully, and had handed out a lot of punishment, but he had never run away when others had retaliated, but now, the first time in years that the fight was for real, he had run away? He couldn`t bear the thought and tried to think of more pleasant things.

However, now that he was fully awake he couldn`t suppress the thoughts that were coming hard and fast. He mustn`t have hurt his assailant that first time because who else would have come after him a second time? Did the chap find a bottle somewhere and come after him to complete what he had tried to do earlier? But the doctor had said that he had been attacked by several chaps. How would the ambulance driver have been able to tell him that? Something was wrong, but he wouldn`t find any answers just lying here thinking about it.

His mind was reeling by now. In that small curtained-off cubicle he was separated from the rest of the world. He was aware of some other noises from outside his little sanctuary, but the comfort of the bed, the blankets tucked in tightly around him and the knowledge that wherever he was, it was a safe place soothed the turmoil inside his head and he gradually sank into a deep sleep.

CHAPTER 3

When Tom contacted the Ordnance Corps RSM to enquire about interviewing the three soldiers he had taken statements from. He was told that as the course they were on meant a full time commitment from them each day, he would have to arrange a meeting during the evening. Tom was keen to talk to them again before he could take Doyle's statement, so he asked to see all three of them the following evening, at half hourly intervals. The first one he met was a Geordie, Corporal Horsfield of the Royal Engineers. He was a regular soldier, twenty-three years of age, and responsible for the Motor Transport duties at the Engineering Services Depot in Worcester.

Tom tried to put the young man at ease by starting to chat about his duties at his depot. Tom knew only too well how wary most soldiers were of Military Police NCO's. Too many of them had a reputation for rough-riding over other regiments and corps, throwing their considerable weight about when conducting any investigations, or even when involved in quite mundane police duties. The response from the sapper corporal was positive, and they were soon chatting as equals.

"I am not looking for another statement from you. This is strictly unofficial. I am just trying to form an opinion about Doyle. I suppose you know by now that the civil police want to question him about the death of the chap he had been arguing with in the pub?"

"Yes, we heard about it from the RSM. But God knows how he could have been responsible for that. He was only out of our sight for a few minutes, and in that time he was attacked twice himself"

Tom had prepared himself for this. "Are you sure you were out of his sight at all? The dead man's mates say that all four of you attacked several of them, concentrating on the chap who died. You kicked him to the ground and then ran."

"Fucking liars", said the corporal, "You saw us on Sunday morning. We were still pissed after that scrumpy we drank. We couldn't have attacked a Chinese meal".

Tom laughed at that. The corporal obviously felt relaxed in his presence to have spoken like that, so he carried on conversationally. "I am not going to go on about that, but I'd like to hear what you thought about Doyle himself."

"He seemed a reasonable chap. Most squaddies think of paratroopers as being right toughs. When I heard Jim's accent, obviously from Glasgow, I thought, 'Jesus, he's like a character straight out of No Mean City, I'll have to watch what I say to him. But he was not like that at all. He wasn't very talkative about what he had done in the army although he did tell us that they were now trying to get him into some cushy job that would keep him out of action for a while. I thought that was because he had been in Northern Ireland. I've heard some stories about that.

I would hate to go there."

"Did he give you the impression that he was violent? You know, like the Glasgow keelies you spoke about?"

"I suppose, like most commando types, there's got to be a harsh streak in him, but he gave no indication to us. Just to pass all the stages of being a paratrooper he must have been helluva fit, and to endure all the things you hear about, even just jumping out of a plane, he can't be a mummy's boy, but violent? I didn't get that impression. That night, he just sat there and drank Coke, and chatted to the girl he was landed with. That's not what I would expect of him. But then, when he shouted out to try and cool things down in the pub there was an authority about the way he did it that seemed to show up his experience. I think he must have had a higher rank at some time. He's used to giving orders- and in critical situations."

Tom was impressed by the corporal's perception. "Maybe you are not far wrong. Did he talk about anything apart from the army?"

"No. But when we got ready to go out that night, he had taken the bed right next to mine, so I saw him close up without his shirt. He's built like a champion boxer. I made some remark about it taking a lot of exercise to get like that, but he just shrugged it off. If I was built like him I'd be showing it off all the time."

"I saw him yesterday. I agree about the physique. I would like it myself."

"How was he? He looked ghastly when we brought him back here. Will he be alright?"

"The doctors are quite hopeful. He was a lucky man. If that bottle had hit him just a wee bit higher he would probably have been blinded for life. As it is the worst thing could be that he will need a couple of false teeth, and carry the scars for a long time."

Tom was pleased with the way that the interview had gone, and sent for the next man. When he arrived, Tom immediately got the impression that he could not have a similar conversation this time. The Lance Corporal from the Durham Light Infantry was a seasoned regular who had been up and down the ranks in the fifteen years' service that he had done. Part of the permanent staff at the regiment's headquarters, he had apparently been told that a good result on the course that was now running could lead to the return of the second stripe that he had lost about a year previously.

When asked why he had been demoted he blamed others for having exposed him as being the leading light in a drunken episode that had finished up with the involvement of the civil police. According to him, his commanding officer had felt obliged to be seen as strict when some shop fronts were ruined by a gang of drunken infantrymen. As the older of the two NCO's in the party he had been made the scapegoat, losing one stripe.

Tom tried to give the impression of being strictly official about the interview, stressing the seriousness of the charge that might face Doyle and the three others if the evidence given by the friends of the dead man was proved to be right.

Lance Corporal Denholm was obviously subdued by the rank and bearing of this MP sergeant who was now suggesting that he might in fact be implicated in a very serious crime, and like the people or person who had shopped him previously, he was quite prepared to help build a case against Doyle.

"I fucking knew that bastard was trouble as soon as I saw him. A right smart Alex. From the start he was telling me what to do. I had to point out to him that he had no rank over me. These bastards with the fancy coloured hats are all the same. They look down their fucking noses at ordinary squaddies."

"He thought he was kidding us, drinking Coke while we all had scrumpy. You should have seen the tart he was with. Nice looking girl, not like the scrubbers the rest of us had. He just wanted to impress her. I know his kind. A fucking Glasgow keely with a razor in his pocket. Waiting to get somebody het up so that he can challenge them. And he did it, didn`t he. He set up that young chap. If he hadn`t said anything, I would have. Englishb Bastards? Who the fuck does he think he is? I would have got my end away last night if it hadn`t been for him. One thing though. He must spend hours in the gym to get a shape like that!"

Tom realized that he was making no headway with this chap. He assumed his most disciplined bearing, rose to his feet and said, "so much for the great companionship between soldiers. I could charge you with slandering Doyle. You went drinking with the man, probably bought each other drinks, had to carry him back to camp when he was so badly injured that he nearly died, and you talk about him like that. You haven`t shown enough compassion to ask how he is. If I have my way I will be recommending to your commanding officer that, for becoming involved in another drunken escapade you should be relieved of your remaining stripe."

"Christ, what got into you? You asked for my opinion of the man, didn`t you?"

Tom finished the conversation at that, and hoped that the next interview would prove more fruitful.

The third chap introduced himself as Corporal Gould of the Tank Corps. A regular soldier in his mid-twenties, he gave the impression of pride in his rank and his regiment. Tom judged him to be closer to the first man he`d interviewed than the second, so started off in the same conversational manner that he had adopted previously.

"There`s nothing official about this. I`ve had your statement. I am just trying to get a feel for this chap Doyle. You know he could be on a serious charge. The police are anxious to pin the death of that young chap on him. What do you think of him" "Well, as long as it`s off the record, I got the impression of a lot of built-up tension in the guy, but he controls it well. I think he is capable of killing someone although I don`t see how he could have murdered that chap. He was almost within sight of us the whole night. How could he possibly have done it?"

"Let`s leave that aside for the moment." said Tom, thinking that he was going to be interested in what this man would have to say. "Just give me your personal opinion. I know you just met him for a few hours, but he must have made some impression." "Right. He is quite an impressive person. With that type you don`t have to hear his story. Anyone that wears that hat has already proved himself. The discipline and the training would break most people. When you hear how he speaks, it is clear where he comes from and that he has not had the benefit of a university education. I actually admire that type. You know, the commando or paratrooper kind. I would have expected him to be a drinker, but if he seriously only drinks soft drinks, I admire him even more. But I don't think I could like him. He'd be a good man to have on your side, but I wouldn't like to fall out with him. Did you see the build on him? He could eat most of us for dinner."

"God, all this after a few hours? He really did impress you", said Tom.

"He did. But I felt a bit scared of him. The only real thing that he did to give me that impression was when he piped up in the pub. What he said was actually quite laughable. Fancy a Scotsman in an English pub saying 'why don't you fucking English bastards just shut up. He was either stupid, or joking, or inviting someone to have a go at him. Personally I got the impression that it was the last. He wouldn't mind how it was taken, but if someone took it as a challenge he knew that he could cope with the situation."

"I know he's not brash but, with the women, I got the impression he was quite shy. He made no effort to get close to any of them." Tom thanked the corporal for his comments, then returned to his quarters, thinking that he had quite a few things to think about. He thought especially how all three that had been with Doyle that night had remarked on his physique. Had that been because Doyle deliberately flaunts his muscles in front of other men, possibly to create some kind of status over them? Most men would have taken the opportunity to preen themselves in front of women rather than men. But Doyle seemed to have made no effort to do so, not even to the prettiest of the women. Had he something against women? Tom resolved to try and find out more about Doyle.

On the following day Tom learned that Doyle would be having the heavier bandages removed from his face, and would probably be able to talk a bit next day. As preparation for seeing Doyle again, Tom paid a further visit to Cove. Not to the camp, but to view the pub, the route that the four soldiers would have taken, and the proximity of the park where the young civilian had been found dead.

He was the first customer of the day at the pub. One look at his uniform was enough to tell the landlord just why he was there. The landlord was a pleasant chap, quite prepared to talk about what he had seen the previous Saturday. "I was surprised when the four soldiers came in, especially in uniorm. When I saw that they were not in the RAOC I realised that they were strangers to the area. We have had trouble in the past with the chaps from that camp, and I thought we`d been put out of bounds."

"They seemed decent enough chaps. I asked if they would like to try our scrumpy. They all tried it, except for one chap who just had a soft drink. Maybe I should have warned them that it is a very potent drink. Even those that drink it regularly can`t manage many pints of that. When four women came into the bar and joined them at their table some of the young locals started jeering at them. It was all lighthearted at first but after a few rounds some of the things that were being said started to get nasty- not from the soldiers, but from our own. Then one of the soldiers shouted out something that got everyone heated up. I might have expected it from one of them who was drinking scrumpy, but it was the other one."

"Well things got a bit fractious, no fighting or anything, but I had to eject one of the locals and then asked the soldiers to leave. They went quite quietly. I`ve already told our local police all this. What happened is shocking, but I can`t tell you anything else."

Tom thanked him for what he had been told, then as he turned to leave the landlord enquired about the injured soldier. When he mentioned that the injured party was the one that had started the row by calling out, the landlord was surprised, saying that he would not have expected that. He thought that Doyle was the one least likely to be involved in any fracas, having given the impression of seniority and stability- despite what he called out. In fact he had thought that it was just some crude joke on the Glaswegians part and had been prepared to laugh it off if the other chap hadn't reacted so violently.

When Tom left the pub to try out the route that would have been taken back to camp he noticed the chip shop where Doyle bought his chips. He also noticed that there was a park which occupied a huge rectangle of ground. The route that he was following, and presumably the same one that the soldiers had used, followed two sides of the rectangle. Late at night the others had probably not appreciated it, but it became clear to Tom that by crossing the park diagonally the soldiers could have cut more than a hundred yards off their journey. The shorter route must have been known to the locals, and Tom supposed that that was how one of them at least must have caught up with Doyle without him realising it.

After he checked on this, he found that the first blood stain, which was still faintly visible, was just beyond the exit for the diagonal path across the park. Tom was then able to picture in his own mind how Doyle could have been caught unawares the first time he was injured, but he could not fathom how Doyle could have killed the other chap and get his body into the park- unless he had killed him before he received that first injury! But if that had happened, the other three must have been lying about the time scale of events. It was obviously important to discover who made the first attack on Doyle, and whether it was the same one who came back for more. Maybe Doyle could clarify some of the questions next day.

He was back at the hospital next morning about 11a.m. Doyle was already sitting up in bed, this time in the secure ward. He looked a lot better with only a few strips of bandage so that Tom got a better look at his face. He actually looked quite handsome. The dark hair was not as severely cut as lots of soldiers. The face was well balanced with high cheek bones and a prominent aquiline nose. His most distinguishing features were his eyes, dark and piercing. His smile was a bit lop-sided, but Tom kept his gaze on the eyes. He could understand the Tank Corps corporal's comment about not wanting to fall out with him. He did not give the impression of being a sympathetic person. Tom asked after his health and then got down to his questioning.

"I've got the statements from the others, and your corroboration of what happened up to the time that you left them to go for chips, so can we take it from there? Just tell me what happened." When Doyle spoke, it was with some difficulty. His upper lip had split vertically into three strips when the blow landed and his nose had had almost been severed from his face. The surgeon had made a very skilful job of stitching the face together again. The stitches all remained, the black knots not entirely hidden by the narrow strips of tape which allowed Doyle to speak carefully. From his position of sitting on a chair that was lower than the bed Doyle was sitting in Tom could see that the nose had been repositioned slightly askew. The right nostril was clearly wider than the left.

From what he had heard from the others, Tom had expected a brash Glasgow accent to go with the hard-man impression, but was surprised when Doyle started talking in an accent that seemed to denote a reasonable education, and more than a hint of soft Irish inflection. Doyle immediately recognized the look on the sergeant's face and said, "You were obviously expecting that fucking awful way that Glaswegians speak. I keep that for when I'm in the barrack room. There's no use talking to them like this. Most of them would think I'm a right softie."

"I was born in Ireland and lived there for about four years before we went to Glasgow, Bearsden actually, and my mother was from England, so there was some pressure to talk correctly." Although Tom was from Edinburgh, he knew that Bearsden was one of the better parts of Glasgow, and when Doyle then revealed that he had attended one of the most renowned Catholic Boys schools in the city he understood where the rather refined Glasgow accent came from. When he thought about it he could understand Doyle's reluctance to retain the gentler accent in the paratrooper's barrack room.

"Just tell me what happened last Saturday. You could be in a lot of trouble, and you might need my help, so don't miss anything." Dole gave a faint smile then started his story. "It's very simple. I went into the chip shop while the others walked ahead, or rather staggered ahead. That stuff they were drinking must have been strong, for after we got in the fresh air they were acting as if they'd had a right skinful. Anyway, I turned down the road to the camp. It was quite dark, there was not much of a moon, and the lampposts were quite a distance apart. I walked about a hundred yards, just eating my chips. There was only one pavement, on the left. I noticed that it was a park on that side, and it looked like some kind of industrial building on the right.

I'd got to about the end of the park when I became aware of somebody coming from behind me, to my right. I was holding the chips in my right hand, but I instinctively pushed my hand and forearm up to protect myself."

"It was like something that we had been practicing week in and week out at unarmed combat for I just seemed to slip into fighting mode. I wanted to protect myself, but at the same time be aggressive. As I turned towards him I got the impression of a big chap with a knife or razor in his hand. Whatever it was, it caught me on the heel of my hand." At this, he held up his bandaged hand and showed Tom just where the blow had landed.

"There was a hell of a pain. I could feel it slicing my hand, but our unarmed combat man would have been proud for I did the movements he has been showing us for years. I swung round on my left foot and gave him a rabbit punch to his throat, and then kicked him in the balls with my right foot. He went down like a sack of potatoes, and I started to run off. I didn't want to be caught near him."

"I don't know how far I ran, but blood was splashing from my hand and I stopped after a while to tie a hanky round it. I was trying to tie the hankie, it was awkward trying to hold it within my teeth, when I heard someone running towards me again. This time he hit me before I could do anything about it. I thought my head had exploded, and I tried to run again, but I could only stagger forward. Next thing I knew, the others had come back for me. And then I found myself in the guardroom at the camp. I felt sick there. I went to the toilet. I stood at the wash-hand basin being sick. I looked up and saw the mirror. There was a big lump on my right cheek, my top lip was in pieces and my nose was hanging off. There was a spray of blood hitting the mirror. I remember thinking that I looked like Charles Laughton in the Hunchback of Notre Dame. And then I fainted. Imagine, a fucking paratrooper, and I fainted. That's the last thing I knew till I woke up here in the hospital. End of story."

Tom had not said a word as he listened to Doyle. Now he asked, "did you recognize the attacker, was it the same chap who had faced up to you in the bar?"

"I couldn't be sure. He was big enough but I didn't get a good look."

"Was it the same chap that hit you the second time?"

A flash of disbelief crossed Doyle's face when Tom asked this.

"It wouldn't say much for my skills at unarmed combat if he could get back up so quickly, would it? I expected him to be out of action for some time. I fact I didn't even look back at him. I was so sure he was out. If my rabbit punch and kick had landed properly he could have been dead. Christ, what am I saying? Someone was found dead, wasn't he?"

Tom was a bit disconcerted at that. He had realised that Doyle had carefully prepared how he described the incidents, but he also had the sneaking feeling that that last remark had been rehearsed as well. The main story sounded authentic enough, but the last bit made him wonder.

Tom was reluctant to go any further on that visit. He felt a bit disturbed. Usually when interviewing soldiers he felt totally in command but this paratrooper had more or less taken things into his own hands. Now, he felt that he was being manipulated. He ended the conversation by telling Doyle that the police inspector would probably be in to see him soon. He advised Doyle to be as candid with the inspector as he had been with him.

CHAPTER 4

The next time Doyle saw Tom he was told that the police would probably abandon the case against him as it had been established that he had been provoked by the dead man and had acted in self defence. However, the sergeant himself still considered that Doyle was guilty of creating the circumstances in which he was attacked, knowing that if he was tackled he had an enormous advantage over any of the youths who had argued with him, an advantage gained from the years of training in self defence as a paratrooper.

If the sergeant had his way Doyle would face a court martial and would face an extended period in a military prison, and discharge from the service. This was a blow to Doyle and he pondered deeply over the situation he was in.

When the sergeant left, and the door was securely locked behind him, Doyle climbed out of his bed. He had discovered during the past few days that by pushing the small ward's furniture to the walls he could create enough room to do the karate exercises that he had been perfecting for so many years. The pyjamas that he wore reminded him of the karate robes that he used to wear when he had attended his classes in Glasgow, before he went into the army. As he had learned to do since he was thirteen years old, he cleared his mind of all the problems that he faced and went into action mode.

The exercises he did had been drilled into him for so long that they required no thought. He could feel the energy flow through him as the various muscles were placed under the kind of strain that had helped build himself up from an under-developed youth to the near perfect athlete he now was. At just an inch under six feet, and weighing nearly twelve stone, he knew that his physique was the envy of many men. If they could have known the effort that had been put into achieving that physique they would probably have been shocked, but in some ways Doyle treated his strict training regime as a sort of penance for the evil thoughts and actions that he was guilty of.

The exercises brought him a brief respite from considering the predicament he was in, but after climbing back into bed, he was immediately thinking again about the situation.

He wondered if the sergeant had delved deeply into his past, apart from his military record. The spot of trouble he had had in Northern Ireland would obviously come up if he were to be tried, but what about those past occasions when he had committed serious offences without attracting the attention of the police. Although he had never been charged by the police, he could not believe that some diligent investigation would not expose him as the common link in a series of bizarre events over the years he had been in Bearsden.

Soon after he had arrived in Scotland from Ireland with his mother, a friend of his Grans' had introduced a young mother to his mother, and he had made friends with her young son, Ross, approximately the same age as himself. Doyle had never had any playmates up till then, having lived in near isolation with his mother and her grandparents on a remote farm near Kilkenny in Ireland. The three adults had doted on him, giving in to his every whim. The introduction of another boy into his life was a rude shock. Having to share toys was not a good thing as far as he was concerned, and it led to early tantrums.

The new friend's mother offered to take Doyle out one day to visit her own mother with her son. Doyle's own mother accepted the offer with some misgivings, knowing her son's recent propensity for argument with his new chum. Ross's grandmother lived on the fourth floor of a tenement block in Glasgow. On their arrival the grandmother gave Ross a rubber ring that she had bought for him. The two boys were left in the kitchen playing with the rubber ring while the two adults went into the living-room to have coffee. The sash window above the sink had been left wide open. Ross pulled a chair up to the sink, stood in it and peed out of the window. Doyle found this hilarious, and went to copy the other boy, but he wouldn't let Doyle up to the sink. He became angry and to spite Ross he picked up the ring and waved it at him. Ross made a grab for the ring and managed to take hold of it. The two boys started to pull on the ring, Doyle on the floor and Ross in the sink. Ross, slightly the bigger of the two, was pulling Doyle hard up against the sink. Doyle spotted his chance and, letting go of the ring, Ross fell backwards out of the window.

Doyle ran out of the kitchen, calling to the boy's mother that Ross had fallen out of the window. The mother and the grandmother became hysterical and ran downstairs to find the boy dead in the back green. He was still clutching the ring in his right hand. When an ambulance arrived the police were notified. They questioned Doyle about what had happened. He told his story and it was accepted by the police as an accident. However, Ross's mother, who had previously seen Doyle in one of his tantrums, protested that her son could not have fallen without some assistance. The mother made it quite plain to Doyle's mother when she took him home that she believed Doyle had pushed her son. Doyle's mother of course pooh-poohed the suggestion and treated Doyle as if he had been involved in an accident himself, showering him with even more care and attention than normal.

There were several incidents at school where he had physically attacked other children in the classroom or on the football field. Many of the offences should have warranted police involvement, but had only resulted in caning by the headmaster and, in a couple of incidents, banishment from the football and rugby teams. What Doyle was not aware of was that at least two of his teachers had recommended psychiatric treatment, but had been overruled by the headmaster. His main concern had been for the reputation of the school, not wishing to alert the authorities to any excessive violence within his domain.

When he had just turned twelve Doyle became friendly with another boy, the first real friend that he had ever had. The new boy, David, was a real street urchin, a year older than Doyle, but slightly smaller in stature, David had recently moved to Bearsden from Glasgow with his father who had separated from his wife. David more or less took

Doyle under his wing, teaching him things that he had never known before. Among other things he spoke to Doyle about sexual matters, which was a completely new subject to Doyle.

On one occasion during the Easter Holiday from school, the boys had gone off on their own to Craigmaddie reservoir, near Milngavie, on their bikes. They parked near the controls on a grassy bank. While they sat there, David resumed his lessons on sex. He had boasted before of his exploits with the girls from his previous street, but Doyle had not believed most of what he said. Doyle himself, due to the constant teachings of his mother, had had very little contact with girls, even those in his class at school. He shunned contact with most people, much preferring his own company. Not yet having reached puberty, he was a shy reserved boy and what David had been trying to teach him had not impressed him at all.

Until then, all David's lessons had been verbal. Now he took it upon himself to teach some of the physical aspects of sex. Doyle didn't want to know any more and asked David to stop. But in continuing to talk about sex, David himself was getting excited, and wouldn't stop his chatter. Doyle thought about the things his mother, and the priest at their church, had taught him about these things, and became increasingly angry.

David then went too far. He tried to get Doyle to undo his trousers. They had been sitting, but Doyle rose to his feet to get away from him. David also climbed to his feet and tried to put his arms round Doyle, but Doyle angrily pushed him aside. David fell to the side where he hit his head on the edge of a stone wall, tumbled over the edge and rolled down the concrete slope into the water. He sank immediately. Doyle, who was a nonswimmer, was still seething at David's crudeness and was not inclined to try and save his friend. He waited for him to reappear, but he never did. When he realized that David had probably drowned he cycled into Milngavie to report the incident to the police. When they returned it took several hours to retrieve his body from the depths of the reservoir.

Just as with the young boy, Ross, the police were unable to prove that it had been anything other than an accident, and Doyle was questioned no further, apart from at the Coroner's court, where a verdict of accidental death was recorded. Only Doyle knew what was in his heart when he had pushed David away. As Doyle thought of his own history, he remembered that shortly after the death of David he had the huge argument with his mother, that had ended in her death. From childhood he had questioned his mother about his father: what was he like: was he tall: where had they lived: why have I no sisters or brothers? His mother had had some stock answers that never varied, which had put him off asking the questions for several years but recently, partly to try and answer the questions David had been asking him, he had renewed his niggling to get answers from his mother. She had not taken kindly to the constant pressing from her son, and frequently lost her temper with him. This hadn't improved their already brittle relationship which depended largely on the calming influence of his Gran, with whom they lived. Gran herself would only give him the same answers as Mary had been giving him so he brooded over it until finally things reached a head.

In the house one day, in July 1958, the arguing suddenly erupted and she made some comments about his father, implying that he had been disposed to violence just like him, even describing Doyle as being "a monster, just like the father". This had been brought on when he had been driven to shaking her violently and pushing his face close to hers. It was as if something had suddenly become clear to her, and he then realised that his mother had not been fooled by his various close escapes from serious punishment. He roughly pushed her aside and stormed off to his room, his heart full of hatred for her. It was the last time he saw her alive. Next morning he left the house early, without breakfast, and stayed away all day. When he returned in the evening, it was to learn that Gran had found his mother dead in bed, apparently from an overdose of the drugs she had been prescribed several months previously. She had been suffering from depression for some time.

He wondered if he had been responsible for the depression, but knew that the blame for her death could be placed entirely upon himself. Strangely, he felt no sorrow for the death of the woman who had brought him into the world, only hatred that she had recognised him for the monster that he was. The coroner's decision that she had died from an overdose of drugs while her mind was disturbed seemed an apt description.

CHAPTER 5

Following the death of his mother, Doyle had gone through a spell of serious angry aggression towards anyone who had dared to cross him. In the time between leaving his primary school and joining his grammar school he began to associate with some other local boys of his own age who played football regularly in the local park. His footballing skills attracted their attention and he was soon playing regularly with them. Although they recognized his ability, he came in for a lot of ridicule about his size, and suffered frequent injuries from tackles by bigger boys. Remembering the trouble he had got into at school, he tried to refrain from any extreme responses to the treatment he was receiving, but he soon abandoned that attitude and set out to show the others that he was as hard, or even harder, than they were. In the tough Glasgow environment that he had become involved in this led to him being recognized as "one of the boys" for the first time in his life.

He had continued to live with Gran in the house that she had inherited from her wealthy husband. She had looked after him well, although she was not a blood relation, having married an uncle of his mother who had been widowed. Her husband had also left her a share in the furniture business in Glasgow that he had set up. The business provided her with an ample income which paid for Doyle's education and ensured his training as an apprentice carpenter in the furniture factory.

Gran had not known the details of Doyle's mother's conception or pregnancy, merely what had been told to her. She looked after Doyle like her own son, despite knowing of the volatile relationship that had existed between him and his mother, especially in the latter part of her life. Doyle himself, incapable of feeling any love for his mother, could not bring himself to love Gran as she deserved, merely appreciated the benefits that she had afforded him.

When he had finished his training in the factory he announced his intention to join the Parachute Regiment. This had disappointed Gran who had envisaged Doyle taking a management role in the business, marrying a nice girl and having a family. To facilitate this she had named him as a beneficiary in her will, leaving him the house in Bearsden. She tried to dissuade him from going into the army, revealing her plans as part of her argument. Doyle would not budge from his own plans, and indeed made other plans of his own. This time he would cold-bloodedly end a life-to gain the inheritance Gran had spoken about. Soon after he went to the army, he stole away one weekend, went to Gran's house from the training camp which was near Glasgow.

Gran was surprised to be wakened in the middle of the night, but welcomed him. While they were sitting in the kitchen talking, Doyle took a rolling pin from the cupboard and struck her viciously on the back of the neck, just above the shoulder. The blow killed her instantly. He then cleared away all the evidence of him having been there. He put on a pair of gloves, set up a stepladder as if he was going to retrieve something from the top of a cupboard. He kicked the steps over, then positioned the body as if Gran had fallen from the steps and struck her head against the edge of a cupboard. He wiped the rolling pin and replaced it in the drawer where he had found it.

He returned to camp without anyone having missed him. When a neighbour called on Gran a few days later she got no answer from her insistent knocking, so called the police. As far as they were concerned, Gran had had an unfortunate accident. The coroner confirmed this when the inquest was held. Doyle was left the house and its contents when her will was read. The balance of her considerable estate was left to the children of her dead husband. Doyle lost no time in instructing the lawyer to find a tenant for the house, and to pay the income into a local bank.

In retrospect, Doyle considered this the best planned crime that he had committed, and frequently congratulated himself on the smooth way his planning had worked out. The success had been a lot more satisfactory than the other deaths and serious injuries he had been responsible for, all of which had been the result of sudden, brief explosions of anger. Now he understood his mother's description of him as a monster. The step from impetuous action to planned cold-blooded action finally convinced him of the truth of the description.

His army career had not involved Doyle in a lot of action, apart from his spell in Northern Ireland in early 1972. As part of the Parachute regiment he had been involved in the infamous action on "Bloody Sunday" in Londonderry. As a full corporal, he had been in charge of a squad of paratroopers who had been positioned in close proximity to the expected finishing point of the planned march by Catholic youths. Doyle had deployed his men to vantage points at windows of some wrecked buildings. He himself had taken up a post within a room that had four windows.

His orders to his troops were that no live ammunition should be used until he ordered it. At first rubber bullets and smoke bombs were fired. When senior commanders became concerned about the response by the seething marchers, the troops were ordered to load live ammunition, but to fire only when the order was given. Doyle himself was crouched within the room, with a clear field of fire through an open window that he faced. At one point, a youth pushed his head above the window cill and saw Doyle. He threw a bottle which struck Doyle, causing him to fire his rifle, and hitting another youth in the thigh. Immediately the remainder of the paratroopers started to fire on the milling crowd of demonstrators, thinking that Doyle had fired under orders.

Many civilians were killed and wounded that day, the most infamous action of the whole Northern Irish troubles, and inquiries into how such a thing could have started were instigated immediately. Back at camp Doyle spoke to the three paratroopers who had been in the room with him. He explained to the others that they all faced interrogation within hours, and he suggested that they should agree on what they said. He proposed that they should all say that they had responded to the first shot that had been fired, whose source they did not know. One of his own troops made it clear that he knew Doyle had fired the first shot. The others agreed with him. Doyle tried to pull rank on them and said that he would place all of them on a charge if they implicated him. Although seen as a good soldier, Doyle was not liked or respected by his men. He stayed aloof from them, never drinking with them and generally throwing his weight around when he had the chance.

When the three of them stressed that they would be giving their own story Doyle went berserk. He fought with all three of them with an anger that took them all by surprise. Although all of them had been trained in unarmed combat, against the years of Karate experience that Doyle had they were like schoolboys. In Karate training no lethal blows are thrown, and the discipline of not landing blows is supreme. But Doyle went into that fight with the intention of hurting, to show his superiority over the others. All of them were badly hurt, two of them with fractures and the other with severe bruising, while Doyle was remarkably free of any damage.

Charges were brought against all of them, but while the three injured men were just confined to barracks for one week, Doyle was stripped of his rank and received a severe reprimand. It was apparent that the Commanding Officer was aware of the reason for the incident, but he could not reveal the true facts for fear of the regiment being blamed for the whole fiasco in Londonderry. Doyle himself, for his own safety as much as anything else, was posted back to the Parachute Regiment headquarters, and reduced to general duties.

That whole incident upset Doyle. He could not bring himself to accept that he had been in the wrong. His action had been instinctive when the bottle had been thrown at him, and he felt that he was being ostracized for nothing. The memory had been with him while he sat in that bar watching the three chaps with him chatting up their women and getting steadily drunk on their scrumpy, while he had been having small talk with the other girl. He would never admit it to the Military Police sergeant, but his idea that Doyle had deliberately contrived to set up a confrontation was not far off the mark. He had been looking for the opportunity to show that he could handle any situation that arose.

Considering that he was now sitting up in bed rueing the fact that he had not expected any of the people in the bar to be armed, it did not reflect well on his ability to handle things properly. But he had come out on top. At least he was only injured- someone else was being buried that very day!

Doyle knew that his behaviour was not normal, that he was not worried when he caused pain to others, and relished situations in which he could cause the pain. He thought very little about other people's feelings, or of their opinions of him. In the years he had lived in Glasgow he had met many men who had tried to give the impression of cold indifference to others. He had had to face up to several of them, in situations where he himself had not been the perpetrator, and had been surprised to have them grovel to him when he displayed his own aggression. So what the hell was there in his make-up that made him the way he was? Was he a throwback to some fierce warrior or some mentally defective criminal criminal? His father would have been the one to talk to, but who was his father?

CHAPTER 6

When Tom got back to his office he made notes of his conversation with Doyle and then he started to reminisce on the career that was soon coming to a close, and the case that he would now like to clarify before he left the service.

He had not gone into the army with the intention of being a military policeman. Born in 1933, he was one of thousands of British boys who would have to do national service in one of the armed forces or work in the mines, when he became 18. He had done well at school, and was expected by his teachers to go on to university, but that would merely have meant delaying the National service, so Tom elected to serve his eighteen months as it was at that time.

He was allocated to the Royal Scots, an infantry Regiment, and duly spent his early training learning the rudimentary things that all soldiers had to learn. In the early selection tests that everyone had to take he was designated as a potential officer but, having come from a very poor background, he could not envisage himself passing through officer training and then live in an Officer's Mess. He was obviously recognised by his superiors as being a cut above most of the infantrymen, and was allocated to clerical duties. This did not suit him at all, and when he became aware of a vacancy in the Regimental Police he asked to be considered for it.

He got the position, was promoted to Lance Corporal, and assumed the role of policeman among the very people he had trained with. Whilst the job effectively separated him from the others, he felt uncomfortable having to carry out policing duties among those he knew. His role meant that he had to report directly to the Regimental Sergeant Major, a distinguished old soldier of many years` experience. The RSM, responsible for all disciplinary matters within the regiment, was not at all the harsh ogre that all the lower ranks understood him to be, and, when things were quiet, used to speak to Tom as if they were equals. He could see Tom`s discomfort in his role, and suggested that Tom might find satisfaction in joining the Military Police as a regular.

Until then, Tom had not thought a lot about his future. He half expected to go into some semi- professional job but was fairly easy about what happened to him. At home he had lived with his mother and a younger sister in a small flat that was barely large enough to accommodate two adults and a near-teenage girl. The prospect of signing on for a period of twenty-two years did not worry Tom. In fact, as he thought about it, he realised he could look forward to an exciting life if he signed up, which he fairly quickly did.

As a Military Policeman, Tom had performed many roles, had taken part in foreign operations, and had dealt with so many criminals that he had lost count. Inevitably, he had come across drunkards, thieves, smugglers, wife beaters, and occasionally murderers. Among the infantrymen he had dealt with there were many tough Scotsmen, all of whom seemed to try to live up to the reputation that had been invented for the characters in gangster movies. Most of them, when challenged, had turned out to be softies, quite prepared to hand out punishment, but unable to take physical punishment themselves. Those who were prepared to take punishment, as well as hand it out, caused the most trouble in an MP's life. Unfortunately, most of them seemed to be Scotsmen, which made Tom Mitchell feel ashamed at times.

From his own experience Tom had found that the lack of fear about injuries to themselves usually went with a lack of conscience about what happened to victims, and an even greater lack of intelligence in considering the consequences of their crimes. Occasionally he had come across apparent thugs who were far more intelligent than they appeared, and when they emerged, they were invariably real thorns in any policeman's side. His early assessment of Jim Doyle was that he was one of the latter. Intelligent, fearless and apparently vicious, he had already shown that he took pleasure in playing cat and mouse with the police.

Tom recalled the apparent lack of emotion in Doyle when he was first told about the death of the young man and the faint expression of disbelief when he had been asked if the same person had carried out the two attacks on him. He reckoned that Doyle knew that the rabbit punch and the kick had both found their mark, and had expected at least to incapacitate his attacker for some time.

Realizing that he was making judgements without any real evidence to corroborate them Tom had to take control of his feelings. It was not usual for him to jump to conclusions, and had learned long ago that he should not let personal feelings prejudice his instinctive fairness in dealing with people. He looked forward to hearing from Inspector Drake after he had interviewed Doyle.

Strangely enough, when Tom met Inspector Drake the following day, the story he got was a lot different from what he had expected. The inspector confirmed that he had seen Doyle, and had listened to virtually the same story as Tom had heard. He did not make any comment on what he had heard, but reported on how his own investigation was progressing.

"We have found splashes of Doyle's blood on the sleeve of the dead man, so it is quite obvious that he was the one that swung the knife or the razor that sliced Doyle's hand. We didn't find any weapon around the site of the attack, so either the dead man or someone else has disposed of it. If Doyle's story is correct, the dead man would hardly be able to dispose of the weapon, and someone would have had to cart a body, or help a badly injured man into the park. There is no evidence of a body having been dragged into the park so it would appear that he had been carried. He was a big chap so two or three, or even more people must have been involved."

"We have statements from the dead mans' friends. There are six of them, all in their late teens and early twenties. They have all obviously agreed on the same story. They all tell about coming out of the pub after your chaps, and then starting to look for their mate. They apparently looked in on the other pubs in town and other places they frequent. They had no joy, so they all went home. The brother of the dead man was the one who phoned me, as I told you before. They all tell the same tale, but I don't believe it"

"The statements that I took from the other three of your chaps were all identical, and none of them would swerve from it. Given the state they were in on the Sunday, they must have been quite drunk the night before. I know what scrumpy can do to you, and I am inclined to believe their story."

"Once I confront the local gang with the evidence I now have, and threaten them with interfering with the evidence by moving a body, disposing of a weapon, and misleading us in our investigation, I am sure one of them will break down and we'll get the right version. That won't get them off the hook of course, for the matter of Doyle's injuries will still have to be sorted out, and Doyle's retaliation against his first attacker will also have to be explained."

Tom was pleased at the inspector's description of how things were progressing, but it did not alleviate his own suspicions of Doyle's intentions when he adopted the aggressive role after being hurt initially.

Inspector Drake came back to Tom just a few days later. He spoke of how he had leaned heavily on the youngest member of the group who had been in the pub when his friend had faced up to Doyle. After stressing the serious position that he was in if he was to be implicated in actually helping to move his friend's body, or to attack Doyle, the young lad, just eighteen years old, broke down and told the whole story.

Six of them had left the pub at the same time as the four soldiers. They left by the back door to avoid meeting the four soldiers, walked across the car park, then entered the park which was separated from the car park by a hedge. The loud-mouthed chap who had been in the pub, was in the park. He informed his mates that he was going to take care of "that ignorant Scottish bastard", showing them the razor that he had pulled from his jacket pocket.

They couldn't dissuade him, and he took off along the path that crossed the park diagonally. The others followed close behind. When they reached the park gate they saw their friend hiding himself behind a bush so that he would not be seen by anyone coming along the pavement on the road that led to the army camp. They all heard drunken voices, and then only three of the soldiers passed the gate, their progress obviously affected by the scrumpy they had been drinking. At that point there was no sign of the Scotsman.

However, just a few minutes later the Scotsman came into view, strolling and eating from a bag of chips that he was carrying in his right hand. As he passed the gate, the chap with the razor ran after him, his brothel creepers making little noise. With the razor in his right hand he swung at the soldier, who was able to deflect the blow with his right hand. All six of the attackers mates then watched in amazement as the soldier abruptly turned round to his left and swung a rabbit punch at their mate's throat. He then kicked out at the other man's groin. Both the punch and the kick seemed to have landed for the attacker fell to the ground as if pole-axed. One of the onlookers was led to exclaim, "Christ, did you see that? It was like some ballet movement."

Doyle did not stay to see how the chap was. He just took off up the road towards the camp. The others ran towards the recumbent figure lying in the road. One of them, the attacker's younger brother, swore and ran after Doyle. He pulled a pint glass from his jacket pocket having obviously armed himself when they left the pub, prepared for some violence. The road was not well lit but they could see Doyle initially running, but then stopping to pull a hankie from his pocket to stem the blood from the cut on his right hand. Doyle's progress was marked by the sound of his army boots ringing on the pavement, but his second attacker made little sound with his crepe-soled wedges. Doyle appeared to be having difficulty in binding his hand, but he seemed to have succeeded. As he straightened up he was attacked for the second time, this time with a blow that was not diverted, delivered from behind and to the right. The two onlookers who had raced after their mate could clearly hear Doyle's scream, and saw Doyle fall forward onto the ground. He didn't stay there for more than a few seconds, then rose and staggered forward.

Doyle's mates must not have been far ahead round the corner for they had apparently heard the scream as well and had come back to see what was happening. The two youths who had been following the brother, grabbed him and pulled him away from the scene of the attack and they all ran back towards the park. While that second attack was taking place the three who had remained at the scene of the first one, had been unable to revive their friend. One of them had picked up the razor that had been dropped nearby, then all three of them lifted the other and carried him into the park. On the way the razor was thrown into a bush. They carried him with some difficulty. He was a big chap, the biggest of them all, and as they were keen not to be seen they carried him away from the path and laid him on the ground. Their efforts at resuscitating him proved useless, and as the others arrived from their chase after Doyle they came to the conclusion that he was dead.

They all started arguing among themselves, while trying to console the dead man's brother, but they then put their heads together and concocted a story for the police, which proved simple.

After their mate had been evicted, they had finished their drinks and then left the pub. they had then gone into the park where they expected to meet the big chap. They had looked about for him and then heard noise from further into the park. There were several drunken voices and then a scream. By the time they came across their friend he was lying on the ground and no sign of anyone else around. They had tried to revive him but to no avail. They had reckoned that once the attacks on the Scotsman were reported, they would be suspected of being implicated. They just left the body in the park and went home, keeping their fingers crossed that the police would go straight for the Scotsman who had caused the argument in the first place.

CHAPTER 7

In the final week of his army career, Tom Mitchell drew up his report on the Doyle affair, as he liked to call it. He would have liked to be around when it was concluded, but he was certainly not going to volunteer any more of his time just to see how it turned out.

On his return to his home town of Edinburgh, Tom had the task of trying to settle into civilian life and build a new career for himself. At forty years old he felt that he still had a few years of work ahead of him, and in the final months in uniform he had been giving a lot of thought to the future. But first he thought of how he had gone into the army and to the Military Police. The first eleven years of his life had been miserable. Brought up in a small dingy flat, he and his mother had suffered badly at the hands of a drunken, gambling father. Fortunately, for them, the father died in a bizarre accident on a building site where he worked as a carpenter. When working close to some demolition work that was being carried out, a beam that was being toppled struck a solitary upright pipe which almost severed the father's head. The mourning for his passing did not last long, and was soon replaced with joy when his employer made a very good settlement on Tom and his mother. At about the same time his mother discovered that she was pregnant.

The family circumstances quickly improved when a larger flat was purchased just a couple of streets away from the hovel they had been living in. Tom was able to continue at the same primary school. A bright boy, he had been in the top ten of his class from the beginning, and in the qualifying exams that he sat when he was twelve he excelled himself by gaining a scholarship to George Heriot's school for boys. This school ran a scholarship scheme for bright boys who had no father. The income from the settlement and the scholarship guaranteed a lot better standard of living than they had known up till then.

The birth of a girl, on whom Tom and his mother doted, ensured a happy adolescence for Tom and a welcome new prospect of life for his mother. In the new circumstances Tom did well in his studies. He kept a high position in his class, but never quite reached the level of being a prospective candidate for university. Knowing that he would become liable for National Service in one of the armed services when he turned eighteen, Tom did not concentrate on thinking about a trade or profession. If anything, he leaned towards one of the professions associated with the construction industry, so when he attended for his medical examination he expressed a wish to join the Royal Engineers. When Tom joined the army he was already more than six feet tall, a lean eleven stones in weight, and very fit from the regular training that he had with his local football team. At one time he had fancied that he could become a professional footballer, but had soon accepted that he was not good enough to play at the highest levels.

He found army life strange at first, but soon settled into the routine. Having to sleep in a large dormitory with about thirty others was his biggest problem, but he got used to the constant snoring noises during the night, and the early rising each morning.

When he took the aptitude tests that all recruits had to take, he was given the rating of `Potential Officer` and faced further tests. Following these further tests he was told that it was unlikely that he could obtain a commission in the Royal Engineers, but he could attend Officer Training College and become an officer in an infantry regiment. This did not appeal to Tom so he renounced the opportunity to try for a commission and completed the long basic training to become a sapper. At the end of his training he remained at the training regiment on the permanent staff. He was subsequently promoted to Lance Corporal and designated to be part of the Regimental Police staff.

The regimental police came under the command of the Regimental Sergeant Major. Tom had to deal with this RSM personally on several occasions. It was with some trepidation that Tom met him for the first time. All RSM`s have a reputationfor being strict disciplinarians, commanding great respect from officers and men alike, but behind the hard shell that he presented to all and sundry Tom found a very approachable man. It probably helped that, like Tom, he was from Edinburgh, and that both of them were supporters of Hearts, one of the two major Edinburgh football teams. It helped a lot to be able to run down Hibernians, the other local team. They often spoke at some length of personal things and when the RSM pushed Tom towards thinking of a career in the army. Tom gave it some thought.

The RSM related lots of army stories to Tom, including some that he had heard from an army friend who was in the Military Police. Eventually, with the RSM`s blessing, Tom applied for a transfer to the Royal Military Police, and agreed to signing up as a regular soldier. One of the strongest arguments that had been put forward for the RMP was that he would not be spending his entire military career in large barrack blocks with hundreds of others. This was because MPs are virtually segregated from other services after their training period is finished.

That training period, which lasted for twenty weeks, at the Police School in Chichester, was an eye opener for Tom. He had further training in military skills, but these sessions were woven into other sessions on driver training, police duties, self and the law. He quickly settled into the rigours of service life and was pleased to be placed high on the attainment list at the end of his training period. On returning home for his first leave, he was proud to have the chevrons of a corporal on his sleeve, but for the first time he wondered about the reception he would get from some of his former pals when they saw the distinctive red cap that he wore as a Military Policeman.

He need not have worried. The physical training that he had gone through, with the natural filling-out of his late teen body, had resulted in him presenting a strong physical presence, as was considered an essential attribute for Military Policemen. This soon cut short any attempt at mickey-taking. His mother had not objected to his move, and she was very proud of the grown man who had come home.

As a former pupil George Heriot's School Tom had kept in touch with the progress of others who had been his contemporaries, through the annual school journal. Having seen that many of them were in senior positions with various banking, commercial and industrial concerns centred in Edinburgh, Tom had thought that he might be able to offer a discreet consultancy in vetting recruits on their behalf. His years in the MP's had given him a good insight into people and he felt confident that he could cash in on his abilities.

The timing of his release from the forces could not have been better, for Edinburgh was in the throes of developing into a large business centre, with many professional companies seeking capable people to fill the huge number of vacancies. Former classmates were delighted to meet Tom again and discuss what he intended to set up. He was given several small commissions that he dealt with effectively, but it was only when he exposed a candidate for a very senior position as having a criminal record during his army days that he made a major breakthrough. Tom's delving into the man's army service record revealed that, while in charge of the inventory at an Engineering Stores Depot, a very large amount of engineering equipment had gone missing. After an enquiry, a team of civilian stock auditors had been dismissed, but the army man had clearly been involved. He was charged and reduced from the rank of Quartermaster- Sergeant to corporal. The company who had been considering the man for a very senior position accepted Tom's report and had not appointed him.

CHAPTER 8

The story of Tom's success on this commission went the rounds of those business men he knew, and did him no end of good for his future. Tom thanked his old colleagues in the Military Police for digging up the information for him, then settled himself into a position that was to become the envy of many.

He had only been running his enquiry agency, as he called it, for just over one year when he noticed a newspaper article in the Edinburgh press about a former paratrooper and black belt Karate instructor, who was about to open a Karate club in a former boxing gymnasium in the City centre. Tom would not normally have paid any attention to such an article, but the name of the instructor, Jim Doyle, rang a bell in Tom's mind. The association of that name with paratrooper might just be a coincidence, but it interested Tom enough to visit the gymnasium. He had heard no mention of Karate when he interviewed a paratrooper called Jim Doyle in his last case as an MP, but that did not put Tom off.

As the gym was only a few hundred yards from the flat that Tom had bought, with his sister, after his demob, he had no distance to travel to find out if it was the Doyle he had met previously. The gym was empty, apart from a well-built man carrying out exercises on his own on a floor mat. Tom had time to watch closely without the chap realizing he was there. He did not think it was the same Doyle. Apart from the same muscular body type, this man had long hair, a moustache and beard, and he wore spectacles. He was about to turn away when the man caught sight of him.

The man's reaction was one of shock, as if he had seen an apparition from the past, and Tom immediately knew that he was in fact looking at the same Doyle. Doyle recovered himself well and made some facetious remark about being able to do without such a shock on his first night in his new venture. Nevertheless, he came forward to shake Tom's hand and welcomed him as his first visitor.

"Welcome to my gym. You are the first one to arrive. And probably the last man I ever expected to see here. But where's your uniform?"

"Oh. I've been out of uniform for more than a year now. I saw the article in the Evening News, and wondered if it could possibly be the same paratrooper Jim Doyle that I'd met in Aldershot. If you hadn't said anything I wouldn't have recognized you"

Was that a look of disappointment that Tom saw on Doyle's face? It was as if he was wishing that he had not come forward so readily. Maybe he had a guilty conscience over the incident in Cove?

"Well, welcome anyway. Did you have any difficulty finding the place?" "No difficulty. But I live just a few hundred yards away anyway. I never expected to see you in these circumstances- whatever happened in Cove? I never heard how it all finished."

Just then another potential client arrived, a youth of about seventeen, thin and undernourished, and obviously nervous, "Hi", he said, "I'm obviously in the right place. I want to join up for karate classes."

"Right. Come on in. If you join, I'll let you have your first year's membership free for being my first customer." "But surely this man was here first", pointing to Tom.

Tom came in then. "I didn't really come in to join. Just to see if this is the same Jim Doyle I used to know. If I'd known I could have had a free membership, I might have said I was here to join. But you grab it. I'm sure you will enjoy it."

Jim Doyle offered to let Tom have a free membership, but Tom thought it was just because the boy was there. The look on Doyle's face when he turned it towards Tom was a lot less than friendly. This did not deter Tom who asked when Doyle would be finished with his class and could they meet up then. "We have got a lot of things to talk about, haven't we?" Doyle recognized that Tom was taking advantage of the boy's presence by suggesting meeting again, and felt trapped into saying, "come around about ten o'clock. We can talk then".

Tom was waiting at the door precisely at ten and watched in amazement when more than a dozen people emerged from the gym. They ranged from youths to well-dressed businessmen, several student types, male and female, and a middle-aged housewife. As they left Doyle invited Tom in. This time they walked right through the gym and entered a flat that appeared to consist of hall, bathroom, lounge, bedroom and kitchen, with a doorway in the hall that was obviously another entrance.

Doyle seemed pleased to show off his home. "What do you think? It was just what I was looking for. Nice and convenient, living above the shop, as it was.

"Wow" said Tom, "How the hell could you afford this? Did you rob a bank?"

"I could be so lucky", said Doyle, "Just after I joined the army my Gran died and left me her place in Glasgow. I rented it out while I was in the army then sold it and bought this place. It was going for a song, the gym and the flat together. It used to belong to someone who ran a boxing club. I even got all his equipment in the price".

"Well, there's obviously a lot of things I didn't learn about you last time we met. You are under no obligation, but could we talk about that? I've wondered how things went after I was demobbed. I thought you might finish up in jail."

"So did I", said Doyle, "but I seemed to have luck on my side, although I had to get out of the mob. I got discharged on medical grounds. I never even got back to see any of my old mates."

"Don't tell me if you don't want to" said Tom, "but I would be interested"

"Right, I'll tell you, but first I'll make a cup of coffee."

When they sat down in the lounge with their coffees Doyle told of how the case had finished up in Aldershot. "I was kept in that secure ward for a while, still under suspicion, but after about a week the police inspector told me that they would not be bringing a case against me. They found my blood on the dead chap's sleeve, so he obviously slashed my hand. When it became obvious that I had just acted in self-defence by hitting out at him, they took into account the unarmed combat training that I had done and decided that I was justified. They found the razor somewhere in the park."

"They even found out that it was the dead man's brother who hit me with a glass. I didn't hang around to find out what happened to him. Apparently, the rest of his pals had carried his body into the park and left him there. They tried to say that we had attacked him in the park, but that was a load of nonsense." "My commanding officer came to see me. He had your report with him. But by that time I had learned that I would have to wear specs for the rest of my life, and I will never get the full use of my right hand again. He said I could stay in the army, but not the Parachute Regiment, or have a medical discharge. That seemed the most sensible thing to do."

Tom had listened in silence. He suspected that there were a lot of things that Doyle was reluctant to talk about, but thought he should not push it too far. Maybe he would get another chance later, but asked about other things. "How come you got your black belt so quickly so that you can be an instructor?"

"It was not so quick. I've been doing Karate since I was about thirteen. I was just one level away from a black belt when I joined up. It took me more than a year after I got out."

"You didn't say anything about that when I spoke to you last." "You didn't ask. Why should I have told you?" Doyle was obviously prepared to be quite belligerent, and Tom knew that if he were to pursue things too far, possibly to the point where they might come to blows, he would not stand a chance with this unarmed combat expert. He changed his tack a bit. "Doesn't your hand keep you back a bit in your Karate?"

"Well, it does a bit, but I'm left-handed so it's not too bad."

Tom realized that there were a lot of things he didn't know about Doyle, and would have loved to go on questioning him, but could sense some irritation in the way he was answering so he decided to call it a day, but tried to leave things open for further talking between them.

"I am sorry about all the questions. I have no right to be asking them. I'd better go. Do you mind if I drop in again? I might even join up with you in one of your classes."

"Come along if you like. The more the merrier." Doyle even managed to make it sound as if he meant it.

After saying goodbye to Doyle, Tom walked the few hundred yards to the flat that he shared with his sister, Margaret. Tom had obtained a mortgage on the property in Montgomery Street soon after he had been demobilised about a year earlier. The area was well known to them as they had been brought up in a tenement building just few streets away. Their new home was quite different from that in which they had lived previously, giving them a large bedroom each, a lounge with a large bay window looking out on a bowling green, and, for the first time in their lives, a separate kitchen, and a bathroom that included a shower. Tom was about twelve years older than Margaret who was now twenty-eight. He had seen very little of her during his years in the army. However, as she had been on her own for several years, living in lodgings following the death of her mother, Tom had met no opposition when he had suggested setting up house together. His army career had not convinced him that he should marry, so was glad to find that Margaret would act as housekeeper in the new home, at least until she found a husband for herself.

Now, as he walked home, Tom was thinking of the conversation that he had with Doyle. In the years that he had spent in the Military Police, he had had to deal with many rogues, thugs and serious criminals, and had come to trust his own judgment. Even during the short time he had spent with Doyle in the Military Hospital in Aldershot, he had formed his own opinion of the young Glaswegian. His accent was a lot more refined than those of the Celtic and Rangers supporters that he had heard at matches he had attended when they were playing one or other of the Edinburgh teams but this cut no ice with Tom.

Beneath the apparent shyness and reserve, Tom suspected that Doyle had a vicious temper and a propensity for violent behaviour. The memory of the case in Aldershot was still clear in Tom's mind, and he was convinced that Doyle was extremely lucky not to be lingering in prison for the death of the young civilian.

On his arrival at his second floor flat Tom was greeted by his young sister. "Will I make you a coffee? Then you can tell me how you got on at that wrestling place."

"Yes. I'll have a coffee, but it's not a wrestling place. It's going to be a gym where the young chap I met is going to set up a Karate club."

"Well, isn't that wrestling?"

"I think Jim Doyle would be a bit upset if I called it that. I looked up some books on Karate. It's one of these martial arts that the Japanese are so famous for. It's more about self defence, personal fitness and discipline than wrestling. You can get all different grades of competence. Doyle told me he had just got his black belt."

Margaret was taken aback. "I`ve heard about black belts. Don`t they give them to the best ones at Judo or Jujitsu or things like that?"

"Exactly, I think they are all variations on the self defence theme. I`m not sure but there must be subtle differences between them all."

"Margaret then turned to the reason that Tom had given for visiting the place in Elm Row. "Was he the same chap you had met before?"

"Yes, it turned out it was. But I don`t think he was very pleased about seeing me there. I probably reminded him of things he would like to forget. You should see the place he`s got there though. It`s right above the Gateway Theatre. Remember it used to be a right flea-pit of a picture- house called the Broadway. Mum would remember it but wouldn`t know the place now. He`s bought what used to be an old boxing gym with a flat next door. I was there once or twice when I was young to get boxing lessons, but Dad wouldn`t pay for them so I had to stop going.

He thought boys should be fighters without any fancy training."

"Well, how was the chap? Didn`t you say it would be a hell of a coincidence if he turned out to be the same person you met before?"

"I did. I knew it was just a shot in the dark, but the article in the News described how the place was to be opened by an ex- paratrooper who had just got his black belt after years in a club in Glasgow. I didn`t know about the Karate, but I had a feeling about that chap. Even though he was just sitting up in bed when I saw him, I thought he was into some sport or other. He just seemed different, even from the other paratroopers I've known. You know that kind of wound-up impression you get of some people. And you should see the body on him. Not like these freaks that do body-building, just the look of fitness you expect in a good athlete. But he's changed a lot. He has grown a beard to hide the scars on his face. His hair i a lot longer and he is wearing glasses. If he hadn't spoken to me I wouldn't have known it was the same guy."

"It seems you were quite impressed by him. That's not like you." "It was only the physique that impressed me. When I first met him I thought that he had just reacted automatically to the chap who attacked him because of his training as a paratrooper, but then I suspected he had wound the guy up, knowing he had a huge advantage over him. Now that I know he is a black belt Karate man I am even surer that he didn't have to hit out hard enough to kill him."

"Tom! You actually know someone who has killed somebody else?"

"Lots of them. That's what soldiers on active service do. The difference with this man is that there was no war on, and I don't think his reaction to the attack needed to be so violent." "Wow" said Margaret, "I'd like to meet this chap sometime." "Right" said Tom, "but just make sure you don't do anything to upset him. I don't want to lose my only sister."

CHAPTER 10

Following that first visit to Doyle's club, Tom waited a few weeks before he returned. During the second visit, on a mid- week evening, he was pleased to see Doyle instructing a class of about sixteen people, male and female, ranging in age from early teens to thirty-something. Tom had been thinking of joining the classes. During his army training he had had to learn basic self- defence techniques and as he had kept himself reasonably fit, he was sure that he could adapt himself again to the physical training.

Doyle welcomed Tom cautiously, and asked if he would like to participate in the class. "I`ll just watch you for a while," said Tom, "It`s a long time since I did anything like this, so let me see what you get up to." The younger man was quite happy about this so turned his attention back to the class.

Tom watched intently. He had been impressed with Doyle's physique when he had met him previously, but now he was able to appreciate the sheer animal-like grace that he displayed when showing his recruits the initial movements that they had to conquer to achieve the first recognition of ability in Karate. He was dressed in the loose-fitting uniform with his hard-won black belt around his waist. Although physically he did not give the impression of being very strong under his uniform, Tom was sure that the relaxed ballet-like movements must have given all his pupils confidence in his right to be teaching them.

Tom watched the class until the end of the lesson and then stayed back to talk to Doyle. `That was quite interesting" he said. I think I will join you. How often do you hold your classes?" "Well, at the moment I am running them three times a week. Monday, Wednesday and Friday evenings. Most of my people just come once a week, but once they become keener, and get used to what I am trying to teach them some of them will want more. The others will continue for a while coming just once a week, mainly so that they can tell their friends what they are doing, and then they will disappear. The keen ones will start to bring their friends and it could start growing. It will take me a while before I am making a living out of this. Just as well that I had my trade to fall back on.`

Tom was interested. "Did you get a good response then from your first adverts?"

`Not bad` said Doyle. "I've got about thirty paying members now, and I'm hoping to do a deal with Edinburgh University. Apparently some of their students are quite keen on setting up a club. We are talking about running club nights on Tuesday and Thursday nights, and on Sunday afternoon. That would be a real break A few keen students between nineteen and twenty-two years old would really set the place up,"

Tom was interested in how relaxed Doyle appeared, compared to their previous meeting, and he remarked upon it. Doyle explained that by describing the tension he had felt on the last occasion they had met.

"I was a bit stressed. It was a big decision to get into something like this when all my life I`d had things done for me. My mother and then my Gran did everything for me, and then in the army there were no worries about money, food, accommodation, even clothes. Suddenly I was here, knew no one, started a business on my own, and when you walked in, I sensed that something had returned from my past. Things are a lot more settled now." When Tom suggested they go for a coffee, Doyle was quick to agree. He sensed that this young man had created a barrier around himself for whatever reason, but in fact needed someone to talk to, at least occasionally. At first both of them were searching for some safe subject between them, talking about Edinburgh, how Doyle was settling in, how he must find the change from Glasgow a bit refreshing, but they knew that the subject of there earlier meetings in Aldershot would have to be aired.

Tom eventually took the bull by the horns. "I must say, I was surprised to see you starting up a club in Edinburgh. It`s funny how your first impressions of people are proved wrong. I thought you were a dyed-in-the-wool regular, and would be for a long time to come. How long were you in the Parachute Regiment?" Doyle obviously thought that the question was without malice, for he answered in a conversational tone. "I was just coming to the end of my third year. I`d signed on as a regular with the option to get out after three years. What happened just speeded up what I think was inevitable. Even if I hadn`t been medically discharged, I think I would have got out."

Tom felt some relief at the reasonable answer and pressed on with the conversation, describing how he had joined up to do National Service and had then decided to make a career of it, finishing up doing twenty-two years.

"Christ, that's a lifetime. Nobody could last that long in the Paras."

Tom expressed interest at that. "Well, I've heard something about the kind of training you have to do, but it doesn't go on like that all the time, does it?"

"You are joking. There is never a week goes by but you're out on some obstacle course or other. The busiest men in the regiment are the Physical Training Instructors. They really keep you up to scratch. Luckily I've been training all my life so I coped with it quite well. I used to pity the poor bastards who came in in a poor state. Lots of them never got past the first few weeks of basic training."

Tom then asked if his only training had been Karate, or was he into some other sport.

"I used to belong to Bellahouston Harriers," said Jim, "I joined them when I was thirteen."

"That's interesting" said Tom, "I used to do a bit of running with Edinburgh Southern Harriers before I joined the mob, but I was never much good. What distance did you run?"

Doyle seemed to be relaxing and answered, "I used to do middle distances. I was never much good at sprinting or long distances but the quarter and the half-mile seemed to suit me. I was always keener on Karate than running. I still run regularly though, to maintain my fitness but haven't been in competition for years, apart from these few army trials that I did."

"What's so good about Karate then?" asked Tom. He had come to realize that Doyle was a lot more complicated person than he had first assumed, and he was keen to keep him talking, but did not want to push too hard. Possibly on another occasion he could bring up the subject of that night in Aldershot to try and get closer to what he thought of as the true story, but tonight he just wanted to keep him talking.

Doyle was quite content to talk about Karate. His enthusiasm for his sport was in direct contrast to the reticence he showed when questioned on more personal subjects. "It's difficult to explain the attraction of Karate" he said, "but the process of learning it occupies the mind a lot more than running does. Running is a matter of fitness, and some technique but nothing like what is required to master Karate. I always treated running as a means of measuring my fitness. When I was at my best I ran fastest, but in Karate a lot of it is in the mind. There is always more to learn, another step up in the grading. You know that I have a black belt, but I'm only a First Dan. You can get up to Tenth Dan!" "A lot of young chaps start in Karate thinking they can learn something to show off to the girls, or to be able to pose as hard men, able to tackle anyone, but the real aim of karate is the perfection of moral character through its training. There is a general acceptance that Karate started in Japan about fifty years ago. The name was certainly adopted in Japan at that time, but really the practice has been in use for centuries."

Tom pressed on with his questioning. "But don't you find it frustrating? I mean, you never actually get to hurt your actual opponents, do you?"

"Well, don`t kid yourself that nobody gets hurt" said Doyle, "the aim is to stop your punches and kicks within an inch of the target, in fact in competition you are judged by how well you manage that, but inevitably some of them land, and if you are not disciplined enough you could deliberately damage an opponent quite severely."

"Some of the things we do could kill people if we went through with them. Some of the punches and kicks would kill if you caught them in the right place, without your opponent even knowing what had hit him. It is the discipline that is so interesting. To push yourself to the ultimate situation, but not go through with it."

"Do you know these moves? Could you kill a man with a single hit?"

"Of course. By the time you get a black belt you are able to break timber planks and concrete blocks by striking them with the edge of your hand. If I were to catch someone with the edge of my hand to his throat or the back of his neck I would cause him a lot of damage. Or look at a kick to the testicles. At the best of times you would temporarily put him out of commission for a while, and if you get it right you would kill him."

Tom took Doyle`s right hand in his own and peered at it closely. "Well, your hand doesn`t look any different from mine, apart from the scar from the cut you had when I first met you." Doyle laughed, "you`re right. But I`m left handed" and he showed Tom his left hand. The striking edge was a solid mass of hard skin. "Besides the trick is to concentrate on hitting whatever is on the other side of your target, so that you go right through with the blow."

Tom did not pursue the matter any further, but he had already made up his mind that he wanted to know this young man a lot better, so he arranged to attend the class due to be held the following Monday. They agreed on the payment and then they spoke of the equipment that would be needed. Doyle assured him that for the first few lessons only loose clothing and bare feet would do. He never suggested to pupils that they shoul invest in the proper equipment until they had really made up their minds that they liked what they were letting themselves in for. After they had parted, Tom walked home, convinced that he was going to find it very interesting to know Doyle better. Already he was starting to consider how he could raise his questions about that unfinished matter when Doyle was hurt in Aldershot. There had been nothing superficial about the injuries he had suffered. The damage to his face, the permanent damage to his eyesight and the vicious wound to his right hand had been evidence enough that he had suffered at the hands of one or more persons, but Tom could not accept, now that he was aware of how capable Jim was at martial arts, that the blows that killed the young Englishman had only been in self-defence.

CHAPTER 11

The biggest difficulty Doyle had in the first year of his new venture, was in developing a friendly attitude towards those who had responded to his advert for membership of Edinburgh's new Karate Club. His mentor at the Glasgow club where he had learned his trade had warned him of the difficulties of becoming a successful trainer, especially in recruiting sufficient numbers to make it a paying proposition,

His background had not endowed him with the easy-going attitude towards strangers that native born Glaswegians all seemed to have, and his own aggressive nature, although now brought largely under control, thanks to the strict discipline imposed by his Karate training, made it difficult to break the ice with new acquaintances. In addition, the cool reserve towards strangers which seemed to be second nature to Edinburgh people, was no help to him at first.

There was one thing however for which he was grateful. The accent that he had acquired from his early years with his English born mother and her Irish grandparents, and subsequently with his mother and Gran Wilsher had not been spoiled by his years of exposure to the rough dialect so common to many Glasgow people, a dialect that was almost abhorrent to Edinburgh citizens. In addition, his evident enthusiasm for his sport and the extremely professional approach to teaching it, soon made his first few recruits warm towards him.

After the first weeding out among his initial recruits, those who had stayed the distance had soon helped to expand the numbers attending the thrice-weekly classes by introducing friends and relatives. He had been nervous about setting up a fee system that might frighten people away, but seemed to have arrived at an acceptable formula very quickly. Each new member was offered a short term membership so that they could assess the value of the classes, and Doyle was delighted to find many are not renowned for turning down bargains, so his long-term advantageous deals were quickly snapped up.

By the end of his first year, Doyle found that he had sufficient numbers to justify setting up several classes, grading members according to individual ability and age. He was especially pleased at the number of children from around ten to twelve years old, recognizing from his own experience that they would learn fastest, would form the backbone of the club for years to come and would acquire high levels of achievement very quickly.

The year had been extremely busy for him as he had been working full time during the week as a furniture maker to ensure a reasonable income. Every Monday, Wednesday and Friday evening had been devoted to organizing his own classes. Latterly he had been instructing Edinburgh University students every Sunday afternoon at their own

Gymnasium, and he had been making weekly trips each Saturday to Glasgow for instruction classes from his old master. He was not satisfied to remain as a First Dan Black Belt holder, so required the additional instruction to ensure his advancement in the grading system.

His former master provided him with the chance of an additional means of income by introducing him to the suppliers of Karate equipment, basically the uniform that everyone wore after becoming regular members of the club. With the number of growing youths, and the frequent damage that uniforms suffered in close work, the sale of the equipment brought him a regular income.

All in all, Doyle considered his first year successful, except in one respect. Although he was not particularly attracted to girls, indeed as he approached his twenty eighth birthday, he had never had a regular girl-friend, he had anticipated becoming friendly with some women of his own age.

Until he had gone into the army, Doyle had had very little to do with girls. From birth his mother had instilled in him so many lessons about keeping away from girls and he had taken the instruction on board completely. Although he had had to share a classroom with boys and girls at his first school, he carefully avoided any meaningful contact with the girls. His secondary education at a boy's school removed the possible temptation of a close relationship with the opposite sex.

This didn't trouble him. He found relief, just as Onin had done, during those years when his testosterone was stirring and by the time he had reached adulthood had more or less resigned himself to a celibate life. Within himself he believed that some day he would find a woman with whom he could have sex and eventually marry, but during his early army life he gave in to the cajoling of some of his mates, and visited a brothel. He was not impressed by the sheer commercialism of his first sexual encounter, wondering what the others found so exciting.

He paid a few more visits to brothels when serving near Hamburg in Germany, but these turned out no better than the first time. However, on the last visit he made with three mates on a weekend visit to the red light district of Antwerp, he selected a beautiful young Far Eastern girl to test the stories of abandonment that he had been hearing from some of his comrades. The encounter threatened to be even worse than any of his other experiences when the girl started to mock him about the size of his manliness. At the time he could not raise an erection, despite the girl's very professional approach to remedying the situation. She had been especially surprised, having thrilled to the display of muscles as he discarded his clothes. Instead of calling it a day, and walking out on the girl, Doyle had become angry, - angry enough to actually hit her several times about the face and bottom. Suddenly he found himself more sexually excited than he had ever felt in his life.

The girl reacted similarly to the punishment he was dealing out and for about twenty minutes they indulged in the most ferocious and sustained sexual session imaginable. When they both collapsed afterwards, the girl professed to being satisfied as no other customer had managed in the few years she had been carrying out her trade- and he was left wondering if he needed to indulge in some form of punishment to reach the kind of climax he achieved on that occasion. The memory of that episode still excited him when he thought about it, but it also frightened him. He was not averse to making people suffer by his actions, and with his fiery temper it was a quite frequent occurrence, but was this how he was to get any sexual pleasure?

CHAPTER 12

Since starting his club, the closest Jim had got to striking up a friendship had been with one of the female students who attended his university class. However, he soon realized that the girl`s flirting was more to stir her male friends than to entice himself, so he did not pursue her for very long. Besides, he had discovered that Karate did not provide sufficient grounding to keep up conversations with decent, sensible young girls, and had virtually reconciled himself to bachelor existence- until the evening of the anniversary of his club`s opening.

He hadn`t recognized the significance of the date when his friend, and pupil, Tom Mitchell, had collared him at the start of a class and announced that they were going to a restaurant in the city centre for a meal. "I knew you wouldn`t remember it is exactly a year tonight since I came here, but I did, and I want you to come with me for a meal to celebrate." Doyle was pleased to bring the class to an early finish, then changed and caught a taxi with Tom to take them to the Old Waverly Hotel in Princes Street. On arrival, they met a young woman whom Tom introduced to Doyle as his sister, Margaret,

Doyle was immediately impressed by this woman who was some couple of years older than himself, but as usual when meeting someone of the opposite sex he was tongue tied. Margaret herself could sense his discomfort and tried to put him at ease. "I've been asking Tom to introduce us for ages. From what he tells me, you are very like him, too tied up in your work, but I've watched him starting to relax far more than he used to, since he met you, so I bullied him into introducing us."

Doyle could only mutter some inane remarks in reply. Tom had spoken of his sister on one or two occasions, and he had formed the opinion of an older woman, a spinster who was happy to live with her brother and look after the domestic affairs. This young woman, a department manager in a large Edinburgh store, as Doyle was to learn within the next few minutes, was certainly an interesting person. She was dressed in an obviously expensive trouser suit which did little to hide her attractive shape, and her auburn hair was rather severely cut in a style that exaggerated the features. Like her brother she was taller than average, only a couple of inches less than his own near six feet, and as they walked into the dining-room Doyle noticed that she attracted the view of many of the men who were dining.

As they were shown to a table, Tom announced, "All the times I've gone out with you, you've drunk coffee. Tonight's a special occasion and we're going to have champagne. Don't disappoint me by not sharing it with us."

At first the conversation was dominated by Tom and Margaret, but after a glass of champagne, Doyle's reserve seemed to melt a bit and he even surprised himself by taking an active part. When Margaret suggested that he must be proud to have had success with his club, he replied, "It's gone even better than I had thought possible. Everything seems to have worked out for me. I'm especially pleased with the place that I have. It is so easily accessible to all my pupils."

Tom had spoken of his sister on one or two occasions, and he had formed the opinion of an older woman, a spinster who was happy to live with her brother and look after the domestic affairs.

This young woman, a department manager in a large Edinburgh store, as Doyle was to learn within the next few minutes, was certainly an interesting person. She was dressed in an obviously expensive trouser suit which did little to hide her attractive shape, and her auburn hair was rather severely cut in a style that exaggerated the features. Like her brother she was taller than average, only a couple of inches less than his own near six feet, and as they walked into the dining-room Doyle noticed that she attracted the view of many of the men who were dining.

As they were shown to a table, Tom announced, "All the times I've gone out with you, you've drunk coffee. Tonight's a special occasion and we're going to have champagne. Don't disappoint me by not sharing it with us."

At first the conversation was dominated by Tom and Margaret, but after a glass of champagne, Doyle's reserve seemed to melt a bit and he even surprised himself by taking an active part. When Margaret suggested that he must be proud to have had success with his club, he replied, "It's gone even better than I had thought possible. Everything seems to have worked out for me. I'm especially pleased with the place that I have. It is so easily accessible to all my pupils."

Tom came in, "Have you ever gone to the theatre underneath your place?"

"No", said Doyle, "Theatres aren't my style. I sometimes go to the cinema, though."

"That's interesting" said Tom, "the Gateway theatre used to be a cinema. It was called the `Broadway`. My mother used to go there when it was called `Pringles Picture Palace`. When they closed the cinema it was used by the Church of Scotland for a while as a Youth Club, just after the war. It was about the first one in Edinburgh where boys and girls could get together under supervision. I used to go there a lot. When Edinburgh started their annual festival, someone had the bright idea of making it into a modern theatre."

Margaret chimed in, "God, where did you learn all this? You've never spoken to me about it. Even though I go there regularly.

They put on some good plays."

Doyle was equally impressed by Tom's knowledge. "It's good to learn something about the place. I just know that my place used to be used as a boxing club. I'm lucky, for it just fits what I needed to set out the mats and give space for exercising." Margaret started to ask about the club and how he was progressing. Tom had warned her that he didn't take kindly to questions about his private life or his sport. A bottle of wine to follow the champagne helped the conversation along. Although Doyle had none of the wine he enjoyed the meal and the company, and was encouraged to talk about how he had achieved his black belt, the ultimate aim of anyone who was involved in Karate. Doyle was not a boastful person, and he didn't hide the fact that he had struggled to master the necessary techniques that formed the basis of the rigorous tests that had to be passed. He had seen others gaining the various colored belts a lot quicker than himself, mainly because he had not immediately grasped the less-physical aspects of Karate, the moral and spiritual development.

When Margaret questioned him about this, he explained that etiquette and manners, emotional strength and character were taken into account in the examiners assessments. Whilst he had found the actual physical aspects straightforward, he admitted to having found it very difficult to learn and practice the mental disciplines.

Much to Tom's surprise, Doyle then revealed that he had only taken up Karate on the advice of a sports master at school because he had difficulty in restraining himself when physically challenged. He even laughingly explained "there must be some right nut-cases among my ancestors, but I am getting better at controlling my aggressive instincts." At that point he realized that the conversation was getting too personal, so he quickly changed the subject, asking Margaret what kind of plays she liked to see at the theatre.

Margaret was pleased to explain that she was hooked on Shakespeare, but as his plays were seldom performed in Edinburgh she contented herself with any serious plays that were put on. She preferred serious plays rather than comedies, listing some of the plays she had seen in the Edinburgh theatres, especially at the Gateway. Doyle managed to show sufficient interest in her conversation for Mary to suggest that, next time a good play was on at the Gateway, she could take him to see it. He had never had such a straightforward proposal for a date from any girl, and he felt so confused that he actually agreed to the suggestion.

Tom was amused at Doyle`s confusion, but silently congratulated Margaret at getting so close to him at such short notice. To cover up for the embarrassment, Tom asked Doyle if he would care to attend a football match with him. "I know we`ve talked about Hearts and Celtic when we`ve had coffee together, but did you know that they are playing this Saturday at Tynecastle? I can get hold of a couple of tickets for the stand if you fancied seeing them."

Doyle surprised Tom for the second time that night as he accepted the invitation, agreeing to meet at two o`clock outside the club on the Saturday afternoon. His usual Saturdays were spent in Glasgow at his old gym, but he was so grateful to Tom and Margaret for the relaxed evening he had just spent with them that he thought it would be churlish not to accept.

As the three of them walked homewards along Princes street and down Leith Street, Doyle felt more relaxed than he had done in a long time. He reflected that he had always enjoyed his chats with Tom when they had gone for coffee together, but that night`s experience had been unlike anything he had ever known before. He even felt pleased that he had gone against his long -held abstinence from alcohol by drinking a glass of champagne. He had felt indebted to Tom for the invitation and had not wished to fling his hospitality back in his face. Besides, he had enjoyed it, especially the way it had freed him from the cursed indifference that was his usual reaction to female company.

They parted company at the end of London Road with Doyle confirming his appointment with Tom on the following Saturday, and Margaret promising to look out for a play that she thought might interest Doyle.

On the Saturday, Doyle duly met Tom, and they boarded a bus to Tynecastle, the home of Heart of Midlothian Football Club. As they approached the ground Doyle was astonished at the number of supporters that were milling around in Gorgie Road, especially the proportion of those who were wearing green and white scarves, the Celtic colours. When they got to their seats in the stand Doyle assessed that almost a third of the total crowd, which was a sell-out, were Celtic supporters. Although he himself had claimed an allegiance towards Celtic, he was not wearing any distinguishing colors-unlike Tom who wore a large maroon rosette in his jacket and a similar colored scarf around his neck.

There were several ribald shouts coming from the crowd before kick-off, including some remarks that could be interpreted as being religiously biased, but there was no indication of any real underlying threat until the match was kicked off. Almost from the first touch of the ball, there were screams from the Hearts supporters like 'get stuck into these Papish bastards' and rather similar ones from the supporters in green and white. One Hearts supporter who was sitting directly in front of Doyle seemed to be one of the worst offenders with screams about the morality of the Celtic players mothers and the legality of their parents marriages. Although not being religious in any way Doyle was quite upset at the invective that was issuing from this person and could barely restrict himself from taking some action against him. Doyle of course was catholic, but gave no evidence of this- at least not at first.

The first half of the match, although exciting, didn't produce any goals, so expectations were still high on both sides when the second half started. Almost immediately after the restart the Hearts centre-forward had a great opportunity to score but made a complete mess of it. The man in front of Doyle jumped to his feet and let loose a mouthful of the most severe condemnation of the Hearts management for having signed `a fucking catholic bastard` who had accepted a bribe to miss against Celtic, following up by calling the center-forward `a fucking Irish whore`s git`. Doyle could not keep his cool any longer and seized the man`s shoulder, telling him that he found his language unacceptable. The man stood up, showing himself to be a lot taller and heavier built than Doyle and asked him if he wanted to do anything about it. Doyle quickly swallowed his anger and refused to become any more involved.

Tom had been watching Doyle closely during the entire match, noting his reaction to the idiot in front of him, and wondered if in fact he had learned to control his feelings away from the Karate mat. Celtic went on to win the match by a single goal, causing his adversary to get even more wild in the things that he was saying, but Doyle said nothing more to him. However, as they were leaving the ground they came upon the same supporter, who immediately faced up to Doyle, threatening him and calling him a `fucking catholic sympathizer`. As Tom watched, Doyle gave this huge man what seemed to be no more than a gentle push out of the way with his left hand, then walked on, but when he looked round the chap was writhing on the ground clutching at his ribs. Tom was in no doubt that Doyle`s `gentle push` had been delivered with all the force that he could summon and that the man would be suffering from badly bruised ribs for some time to come. No one else around had seemed to notice what had happened.

CHAPTER 13

It was several weeks before Margaret was in touch with Doyle again about going to see a play with her. She described how the Gateway did not seem to be having anything suitable, but she had reserved two seats for a play at the Royal Lyceum theatre, for the following week. Although Doyle realized immediately that he would have no classes on that night, his first reaction was to put her off. He had enjoyed her company at dinner with her brother, but, as he admitted to himself, he was almost terrified at the prospect of spending an evening alone with a nice looking woman. His few attempts at dating had all resulted in embarrassment on both sides, on the girl`s side because she could not get past the cold exterior that Doyle always presented to people, and on his side because he believed the stories that he had heard on numerous occasions about girls who flung themselves at boys to trap them into marriage.

Sex had never been high on Doyle`s list of priorities. He fantasised about girls, and took the usual easy way of relief that boys have always used, but since coming out of his teens he had very little inclination to keep indulging in that.

Now, halfway through his twenty-seventh year, he did not know how he would cope with a relationship with a lovely gregarious and, he suspected, sexually experienced woman who was just a couple of years older than himself. He had watched Margaret closely during the meal they had together and had listened intently to her conversation. He was not so stupid, or naïve, to believe that she was anything other than a healthy, intelligent, well -educated woman, and that it had been her who had pushed her brother into the dinner situation, because she had been intrigued by what Tom had told her about him.

Despite his misgivings, Jim accepted the theatre invitation. As he didn't know the theatre, Margaret described where it was, and arranged to meet him there about quarter of an hour before the show was due to begin. Feeling very nervous, he left his flat with plenty of time to spare and walked by Leith Street and Princes Street to the West End, turning up Lothian Road and into Castle Terrace. He seldom visited this part of Edinburgh, so he appreciated the fine Victorian building that housed the theatre, and the vast imposing view of Edinburgh Castle which dominated the skyline just a few hundred yards away.

For the occasion he wore his only suit, which was dark grey, a white shirt that he had bought that day, and a smart striped tie that went very well with the rest of his ensemble. He had even visited a hairdresser to have his beard and moustache trimmed, and the unruly mass of hair tidied. Having only seen Doyle in very casual clothes, Margaret almost walked past him in the theatre foyer, and it was he who came forward when he saw her. She was wearing high heels that brought her up to the same height as Jim, a tweedy skirt that fell just below her knee, what looked to be a cream colored silk blouse and a jacket which hung loosely, exaggerating her shapely bust. He hoped she would not embarrass him by pecking him on the cheek, and she seemed to read his thoughts for she extended her hand to shake his, saying

"hello Jim, it`s nice to see you again,"

Doyle had been rehearsing all day how he would greet Margaret, but his almost chronic shyness took over. He could only manage "thank you", blushing furiously. He need not have worried.

Margaret had assessed him correctly on their first meeting, and realised that initially it would be up to her to relieve the tension of the occasion.

"I`ve been looking out for a play that I thought you`d appreciate, but this is the first one that has come up. Do you like Alan Ayckbourn?"

"I`ve never heard of him"

"Wow, we really do have to start from scratch, don`t we? Well, he`s been around a few years now. He writes mainly comedy plays, they are still serious, but you get a laugh as well."

Doyle could see that Margaret was as nervous as he was, but he could also appreciate the effort she was putting in to try and make him feel more relaxed. She then spoke about the theatre they were in, explaining that it was nearly a hundred years old and had a long history of having put on successful plays, in which some of the most famous British actors ever had taken part. She also spoke of how the highest level gallery was no longer used, and was reputed to be haunted by a ghost. This made him smile, and as they walked towards the auditorium he began to feel more relaxed. At one point they passed a large mirror, and as Margaret spoke to him he turned so that he could see their reflection in the mirror. What he saw sent a thrill of excitement through him, recognizing the two of them as a very striking couple, he tall, slim and athletic looking, she equally tall, elegant and extremely sophisticated.

Before they settled into their seats, Margaret pointed out the reputedly haunted gallery and the many architectural features of the old theatre, then the curtain went up. Jim had anticipated total boredom at this, the first stage play he had ever seen, but he was pleasantly surprised to find that he understood the dialogue clearly, recognized the comedy when it was revealed and appreciated the performance of each of the main actors. By the time the interval arrived he found himself laughing along with the rest of the audience at the near slapstick parts, and he clapped enthusiastically when the curtain went down on the first act.

Margaret, on her part, had awaited Doyle's reaction with trepidation. She had selected this play carefully. She knew that so many modern plays were full of sexual innuendo, and had rejected all those that had been put on at the Gateway for this reason, suspecting that such a play would embarrass Jim too much. The comedy was obviously just right for breaking the ice between them.

Doyle was clearly more relaxed as they went to the bar in the foyer at the interval and made some comments about the play. Margaret felt some satisfaction at his reaction, but was disappointed when he would only have coffee from the bar. She joined him in having a coffee, despite feeling that she deserved a good gin and tonic, or a glass of wine, to relieve some of the tension she still felt. She was a sophisticated woman, quite used to male company, but this strange serious man, no longer a boy, was testing her resilience to near breaking point. She had been impressed by what her brother had told her about Doyle, and had pushed him into the dinner date that they had had, becoming interested enough in him to have suggested the theatre visit, but she wondered if their relationship was going to go anywhere. She had dressed deliberately to show off her legs and her shape, thinking that she was bound to awaken some kind of response from Jim, but he had hardly taken notice of her before they entered the theatre, and she was already making up her mind that if there was no improvement before the evening finished, this first date was also going to be the last.

The remainder of the show passed off successfully, and as they left the theatre Doyle thanked Margaret for the invitation and praised her choice of play. "I don`t think I could have stood a Shakespeare play or some heavy dramatic show. That was very easy to understand. I really enjoyed it." He then suggested walking along Princes Street, on the gardens side. The evening was clear but a bit cool and they walked leisurely, talking about the play they had just seen. Margaret tried to draw out of Jim an opinion on the various actors, but he wouldn`t be drawn, pleading that he had no basis on which to judge the various performances, just repeating the enjoyment he had got from it. Margaret felt as if she was having to plod through thick mud, she was getting so little animated response from him, and suggested that they go for a drink. Again she was disappointed when Doyle expressed a preference for coffee instead of an alcoholic drink as she wanted, and felt she was getting even closer to giving up any hope she had for a relationship with him.

Once installed in a café, Margaret tried several leads to get Jim talking. Any personal questions were easily brushed aside, until she asked about his schooling. When he mentioned the name of the Glasgow secondary he had attended, Margaret immediately recognized it as a leading Roman Catholic school for boys only and suddenly began to realize where at least some of his diffidence towards her had come from. She also realized that she would still have to pick her questions carefully, avoiding questions about girls.

She therefore asked about the subjects he had liked, the sports that he had played and the teachers he had had. Jim responded well, describing how he had excelled at Maths and at languages, but had never had any interest in English, hence his lack of knowledge on Shakespeare and other playwrights. Margaret at last felt that they had something to talk about so pushed him for some stories about his rugby which he professed to have loved but had given up fairly early. On being pressed he admitted to having been a scrum half when he was young, explaining that until he had taken up karate and had started training regularly, he had been undersized, the virtual nine-stone weakling that had been made famous by Charles Atlas.

She expressed disbelief, commenting on his height and his physique, but he assured her that he had been small, and that, like many small men he had been very aggressive, so much so that he had been banned from rugby for having hurt another player very badly, putting him in hospital. He also explained how that incident had led him to join an athletic and a Karate club, both of which helped him to develop.

He described how he had joined a karate club that one of his teachers belonged to. It was not well organised, but he loved it right away, and when the first real karate school opened in Glasgow by the first Scottish Black Belt he had joined. The trainer there, Tim Dexter, had really taught him all he knew, and had encouraged him to set up his own club.

Margaret realised she was not going to learn any more about Jim that night, but what she had learned before they parted encouraged her to think that there was a chance that a friendship could develop, so when he gave her a very chaste kiss at the door to her apartment she agreed to see him again if another play that she thought suitable came to Edinburgh.

CHAPTER 14

Following the dinner with Doyle, Tom pushed a bit harder to form a better relationship with him. Instead of going for a coffee after the karate class, Tom took to spending an hour or two at the gym on his own with Doyle at least once a week. In addition the two of them frequently went out running together. Gradually Tom had started asking more personal questions of him. He started by enlarging on what he already knew.

"Considering your devotion to Karate, it seems strange that you went into the army. How could you tear yourself away from your sport, especially when you were so close to your black belt?" Doyle's reply surprised Tom. "Well, like most young chaps that take an active part in sport, I had a hero that I virtually worshipped. After my sports master at school introduced me to a group of chaps who were learning karate, I got quite interested, and then someone brought this chap along to one of our training nights. He was streets ahead of any of our chaps, and he was about to start a karate club of his own in Glasgow. We all joined it. I thought the man, Tim Dexter, was great. He became the first black belt karate man in Scotland." "'But what had that to do with the army?"

"When our classes were finished, I used to stay back and give Tim a hand to clear up in the club. We used to get chatting. I had never known a father or a grandfather. My mother was dead and I lived with my Gran. This was the first time I ever had an adult male to talk to on equal terms, and he used to tell me stories about how he had practiced Karate on his own, and how he had joined the Parachute Regiment TA unit. He had qualified as a commando and as a paratrooper."

"I could speak to him about anything, and he suggested that when I finished my apprenticeship in the furniture trade, I should think about going into the army for a while. He claimed that I had an aptitude for the sport, especially the technical side of it, but as I had known myself for some time, he thought I should concentrate on the moral and spiritual side of Karate. He thought that the discipline that I would encounter, and the companionship that was inevitable, would be very much to my advantage if I wanted to progress. Even then he was trying to convince me to carry on with Karate and learn to be an instructor. At Karate you don't mature in your early twenties, it takes years to get to the top levels, and a couple of years out of the mainstream does no harm. So that's why I joined the Parachute Regiment."

"Well, did it work?" asked Tom. 'Do you think you are a better man because of it?"

'I am certainly fitter than I have ever been before. The training you get is fantastic, and you learn about discipline. These first few months, I had to keep restraining myself from getting into trouble with the NCO's. Seeing the punishment that was handed out helped with that of course. And in the army, as you know, punishment is immediate. No waiting for a date at court. Just appear before your CO next morning and accept your punishment like a schoolboy. Despite that I liked those first few months. Jumping out of a plane is something special. The worst times though were when we were on duty in Northern Ireland` "It was probably worse for me than most of them for I`m a catholic, and you can take it for granted that a lot of those stories about how British troops had vendettas against the young thugs are correct. It was depressing at times to have to face up to the gangs, but my second spell there was the worst. That Black Sunday as they call it was like real warfare, bullets flying about, civilians being shot, and knowing that our own lads were as much responsible as anyone else made me crawl. I did my share of shooting, but I felt no pride in it."

"Normally, on border patrols and seeking out the IRA supporters, I took as much pleasure as anyone from handing out beatings, but it repelled me to be firing at them. It was partly what had happened there that convinced me to get out at the first opportunity. In a queer way that bastard who hit me with the glass did me a good turn. But you must have been in Northern Ireland, you got out about the same time as I did, so you must have been there."

Tom agreed that he had had one spell of duty there, but pointed out that as an MP he didn`t become involved in the duties that an infantry regiment would get, but he had had to investigate many incidents in which troops were suspected of having assaulted civilians. He had not enjoyed his time there, and had been happy to be posted to Aldershot to finish out his time.

What he did not tell Doyle was that in his spell in Northern Ireland, there had been several incidents that he had had to investigate, in which British soldiers had been accused of dealing out punishment to young IRA sympathizers. In many of the cases, Tom had gathered sufficient evidence to justify prosecution of individuals and groups of soldiers but there had been decided reluctance to avoid charges against the culprits, on the basis that the publicity would just be playing into the hands of the IRA, ensuring them even stronger civilian support.

Tom had felt frustrated at these times, especially as he thought that this made a mockery of justice, and encouraged the widespread use of punishment on what was frequently innocent Irish youths. He did not consider himself particularly moralistic, but he did think that if a crime is committed, and is seen to be committed, then the culprits should face a trial. He was mostly upset by the number of cases of assault that had involved the Paratroop Regiment and the SAS, who often appeared to be trying to live up to the hard reputation that they had established for themselves. And Doyle had belonged to that group.

In the classes that Tom attended, there were several boys in their early teens. In view of what Doyle had said about the less physical aspects of Karate, Tom started to take a keen interest in three of these youths. It was quite apparent that they were close companions, but Tom also guessed that the smallest of the three was bullied by the other two. Even during the early classes the two bigger boys kept on at the smaller one, aided now by what they were learning about Karate holds and moves, but Tom could also distinguish that the small boy was apparently learning faster than the others, for he was showing more confidence in handling himself, and could successfully counter what the others tried to do to him, frequently imposing punishment of his own. Although the relationship between the three boys must have been evident to everyone in the class, including the tutor, Tom was surprised that Doyle did not make any effort to avert the bullying. One evening, after the class, during which the three youths had been indulging in some tomfoolery, the smaller one clearly reached the end of his tether and dealt both of his tormentors a series of blows that obviously hurt, Tom asked Doyle why he had not admonished any of the three. "That little fracas between the three boys was hardly what I expected here. Why did you not stop it? They have been building up to that for weeks. Could you not see it coming?"

"I'm not indifferent to what happens in my classes" said Doyle.

"I see everything that's going on, even in a class of fifteen to twenty. It's been clear what was going to happen sometime. If I had thought someone was going to be badly hurt I wouldn't have let it happen, but Ian, the smallest boy, and clearly the best of the three, doesn't know enough and isn't yet strong enough to do the others a lot of damage, so I let it happen. It is all part of the training."

"In the next class, I'll be able to recall that incident, and build on it to stress the need to control your feelings, even under stressful conditions. That is just as important if you are going to succeed in Karate. I have watched these boys since they first came here. Ian reminded me of myself when I first started. At that time I had been a bully myself, just by being the toughest of the boys I was at school with, but when

I started Karate, I was the youngest, and the smallest in my group, and I got bullied by a couple of the bigger boys, both typical Glasgow thugs who had actually joined the class to learn new ways of developing their "hard men" reputations. I took their bullying and tried to control my temper, but one night they went too far and I just blew it. I did remember the holds and blows that we had been learning and I used them, but did not hold back. The tutor banned all of us from the club." "I stayed away for a couple of weeks then went back and asked to be reinstated. The other two were not there. I got my ex- teacher to plead with the master on my behalf. He finally gave in but warned me that if there was any more nonsense I would be out on my neck. He stressed the need to control myself if I was to go on at Karate, for which he thought I had an aptitude."

Tom accepted the logic of what Doyle had told him, but it made him wonder about how well he was actually able to control his temper. The incident after the match at Tynecastle was still fresh in Tom`s mind, and he felt sure that he had witnessed a callous, though discreet assault on someone who had merely annoyed Doyle. By now, he was aware of the blossoming relationship between Doyle and his sister and he wondered if he should make some comment to her about what he`d witnessed at the football match. He decided to keep the incident to himself, but determined to keep a close eye on Jim to see if any other incidents occurred.

In fact, it was Margaret who reported on something that made Tom suspect that there was a cruel streak in the young man she was cultivating as a theatre-goer. After one night out she described to Tom how she and Doyle had been walking home that evening after seeing a show when they passed a pub in Lothian Road which was disgorging drinkers at closing time. One very aggressive drunk had confronted the two of them and used some foul language to Margaret. Doyle had hardly broken step, but had dealt a single blow with the side of his left hand to the base of the drunk's neck. As they walked on Margaret turned back to see whether the man's friends were coming after them, but saw only the one man squirming on the ground.

CHAPTER 15

As his second year in Edinburgh unfolded, Jim found himself seeing more and more of Margaret. Their friendship continued to be completely platonic, as if the two of them had agreed not to push things too fast between them. Margaret had been assessing Jim closely during the entire year, and had concluded that, if she were to be the one who made some kind of sexual proposal, he would take fright and run. She didn't want that to happen as she had found many things to appreciate in their friendship. Jim was never less than gracious towards her, indeed from a very early stage in their relationship he had sent flowers after each theatre visit, pecked her cheek when they met, and escorted her to her door at the end of each date. He made her feel safe and coveted, without ever expressing truly romantic phrases, had never been in her flat, or on his own with her in his own flat.

Margaret's job as manageress of the Women's Clothing Department of the new Edinburgh store of John Lewis entitled her to substantial discounts on all the store's goods, and she had passed on many bargains to Jim during that first year of their friendship. His flat was furnished in the most up-to-date style, his kitchen equipped with the latest continental appliances, and she had influenced Jim very strongly to wear the most fashionable men's clothing on their frequent visits to the theatre and on their regular walks around the historic parts of Edinburgh. Alas, none of her efforts to get really close to him, and into his bed, had paid off.

Margaret herself was no virgin. She had had several serious relationships but none of them had reached the marriage stakes.

Even during the year that she had known Jim, she had continued to see other men and had enjoyed a satisfactory sex life as many single, independent young business women did, without commitment on either side, and no recriminations when the relationships ended. She would have welcomed any advances that Jim made, but was content to go along with his apparent lack of need for physical attachment.

Their conversations had improved considerably since their first couple of meetings, with Jim gradually revealing details of his past, but she did not feel close enough to him yet to discuss really personal matters. He had disclosed few details of the life he had lived with his mother, and Margaret had concluded that some dark secret had been withheld from him, a secret that had played an important part in his mother's attempt to shield Jim from life's difficulties, and its joys.

Margaret herself had been brought up almost entirely by her mother, who had been into her forties when Margaret had been conceived, and just a couple of months older when her husband had lost his life in a building site accident. With her mother she had a very close relationship, despite the huge gulf in their ages. She had been encouraged to cultivate her own independence, probably as a reaction to the stifled existence her mother had endured while her husband had been with her, and as a result her childhood and her youth had been very happy. At her primary school she had done extremely well, gaining a scholarship to the renowned Gillespie's Girls School in Edinburgh. The financial return from the scholarship, and the regular payment that her brother made from his army allowance meant that she never experienced the drastic poverty that Tom had known throughout his own childhood.

She had hardly known her brother before he had gone to the army, but became close to him on his frequent leaves, even more so as she grew into her teens. Their relationship, despite the age gap between them, was closer than she would ever have attained with the drunken father she had never known. Since joining Tom in the purchase of a flat, they had enjoyed an easy-going relationship, placing no restrictions on each other's use of the premises for dining or love-making when the occasion demanded, and sharing quiet evenings and weekends when no others were around.

If Margaret had wished to bring Jim home to share her bed on occasions, Tom would have raised no objections. In the absence of any such wish, Tom had assumed, knowing that they were seeing each other frequently, that the relationship between Margaret and Jim was sexual, and that they shared Jim's own bed at times. Margaret had no inclination to enlighten Tom on the exact nature of the relationship.

The few snippets that Jim revealed about his mother intrigued Margaret. As far she could gather, Jim was born when his mother was very young. It had been hinted to him that she had married a distant cousin who had come from Ireland to seek work, but had died in a tragic accident soon after she had discovered she was pregnant. She had some kind of mental breakdown after the loss of her husband and had never fully recovered.

Jim was born in Ireland and had been brought to Glasgow when he was only four years old, and he was only twelve when his mother died, after she had suffered some kind of relapse. Jim had no details of his grandparents on either side, although he had been told that his mother had lived in Coventry at one time with her parents and a sister. The woman with whom he had lived after his arrival in Glasgow, although known to him as Gran had apparently been the second wife of the widowed husband of her grandmother's sister, therefore totally unrelated to Jim or his mother.

Jim appreciated the relationship that had existed between his mother and Gran, and was especially grateful that after his mother had died Gran treated him as if he was a full blood relation, even leaving him the grand house in Bearsden, in Glasgow, when she died. While in the army he had rented the property out, and had invested the money sensibly. On his release he had sold the house to finance his purchase of the gym. Margaret was impressed by Jim's story. From their first meeting, indeed from the stories that she'd heard from her brother before she was introduced to Jim, Margaret built up the picture of a considerate, thoughtful young man, a bit embittered by what fate had thrown at him, but nevertheless trying to adjust his life and those of the pupils who looked towards him for training in Karate. She had no illusions that he was entirely soft-hearted, to have achieved his distinction in athletics and in Karate was evidence enough of a steely resolve within him, as was his application towards making a success of his new venture. It was clear that his concentration on his chosen sports had limited his interest in girls, and what Margaret herself considered the finer things of life, such as music, literature and theatre. Thankfully her own efforts in the past year had led him to at least make a token gesture towards acquiring a belated introduction to these pastimes. He didn't argue when Margaret suggested some books to read, some music to listen to, and plays to see at the theatre, and was quite prepared to discuss these various subjects, albeit at a very elementary level, when they did have a date. So although Margaret could not get him to reveal much about himself, she was pleased that she had managed to get him to take part in sensible conversation.

Frequently Margaret talked about Jim with her brother, until Tom recognized that she was taking a greater interest in him than he had seen her do towards any of the other boyfriends he had been introduced to. He himself remained a bit wary about getting too close, for he suspected hidden depths to the younger man, depths into which he had no particular desire to delve. He felt sure that Doyle kept silent much of the time because he did not want to reveal some inner secrets, and that his non-drinking was part of the defenses that he had erected. Tom remembered the dinner that the three of them had had together, and how one glass of champagne had helped to loosen Doyle's tongue far more than at any other time with Tom. He also recalled the incident at the football match when Doyle had struck someone without a great deal of provocation.

As he watched the friendship between Margaret and Doyle develop, Tom realized that marriage was a distinct possibility, but the prospect did not please him. Despite having known Jim for two years, Tom felt that Doyle was still very much a stranger. There was seldom much exchange of intimate information between them. They spoke about Karate, especially now that Tom himself had started to achieve various colored belts, thanks to the one on one sessions that he had been having in the gym; about football when Tom could persuade Doyle to accompany him to Tynecastle; and on their weekly coffee hour after Wednesday training sessions, but Tom found great difficulty in extracting any real facts about where he had come from. This was particularly frustrating to Tom as the greatest part of his professional life was now spent in checking out on potential employees for some of Edinburgh's expanding financial companies. He therefore determined to make a strong effort to check on Doyle's background before he was asked to give his blessing to a wedding, as he felt sure he would be asked to do in the near future.

CHAPTER 16

To get a starting point for his investigation, Tom tried to get some personal information about Doyle from Margaret, but she could not provide him with much guidance. It seemed to Tom that Doyle had deliberately avoided ever talking about his past for fear of some dark secret that might be revealed, so Tom decided to start off at the only point that he had given any indication of- the man whom Jim had considered his hero, Tim Dexter, the Karate instructor.

Tom had no difficulty in finding a route to Tim Dexter. Just a few inquiries revealed that this man was the acknowledged head man in Scotland for Karate. In addition to the administrative role that he played in the sport, he was also the leader of the team that was already making a strong reputation for itself in international events.

A phone call to Tim Dexter was sufficient to arrange a meeting at the master's gym, especially when Tom explained what he was after. Tom was no stranger to Glasgow, and easily found his way to the address he had been given. His first reaction on meeting Tim Dexter was that he was just an older version of Doyle, the same suppressed energy, the taut muscles that strained against his close fitting T-shirt, and the impression of a man who was completely in charge of his physical space. Tom had done some checking up on Tim's background and he had been most impressed.

Tom was welcomed by the master who quickly established that Tom was in fact a pupil of Doyle's, but that his visit was not to discuss Karate. He was quite blunt as he described what had prompted him to come to Glasgow. "I've been training under Doyle since he opened in Edinburgh. Although we are quite friendly I feel I hardly know him. But about a year ago I introduced him to my sister, they seem to be getting close and I suspect they will soon be thinking of getting married. My sister is a lot younger than me, and I am like a father to her. I'd like to know a bit more about the man she is likely to marry, but I don't know where else to turn to. Jim doesn't reveal a lot about his life before he arrived in Edinburgh, and I'd like to fill in some gaps, like who are his parents, has he been in trouble, indeed, has he been married before? He has spoken to me about you before. I'd say he nearly worships you, and I wondered if you could give me any leads towards knowing him a bit better?"

Tim Dexter did not appear to be surprised by Tom's questions, although he did try to play down Doyle's opinion of himself. "I just happened to be around when Jim needed someone to set him straight. I suppose we got on alright from the time his teacher brought him to my classes. But I don't think anyone got close enough to him to know his life story. His teacher, Father O'Malley, ran the rugby at Jim's school. He thought highly of Jim as a potential rugby player, but had trouble controlling his temper. He didn't take kindly to being disciplined, then started handing out the rough stuff. Eventually he ended up hurting an opponent quite badly, enough to put him in hospital, and the father banned him from the team."

"It was strange, for you think of rugby players as big chaps, but Jim was quite puny when he first came here, although you'd hardly believe it now, but he'd face up to anyone, no matter what size he was. The father was in a Karate club that I knew about, and he brought Jim to see me, even joined my club himself when I said I would take Jim. He was a right hard nut at that time, trying to live up to his reputation, and I thought it would be a right challenge to get him to toe the line, not that I had much confidence in doing that."

"You know the reputation that Glasgow hard men have. I have seen so many of them, even had them in my club. But most of them don't last long. When they discover that I'm trying to teach them to learn about personal control, they are not so keen. Most of them just learn some of the basic moves and exercises then go away to show off what they have learned. Jim was not like that, though. He really tried hard, and was progressing well, but after a few months I had to ban him from the club. He had been getting pestered by a couple of so-called hard men, just bullies really, but one night he couldn't take any more and went nearly berserk. It was lovely to watch, for he did all the right moves, but didn't hold back from hurting these two. I actually felt proud that one of my pupils had learned so much in such a short time but I had no alternative but to bar him from the club. The other two never came back, but after about a month Jim came back to apologize, and begged to get back. He promised to control himself a bit better so I gave him one further chance. From then on he handled himself well. There were times when I thought he would blow it again and I had to tick him off by refusing his advance to higher grades, but he knuckled down well. He is an excellent karate man now".

Tom was impressed by what he was hearing, but kept on with his questioning. "But what about his parents? Do you know anything about them?"

"I just know that his mother died before he came to my club. I never heard him talking about his father. He lived with his grandmother. I believe she's dead now."

This didn't clarify anything as far as Tom was concerned so he then asked about the teacher who had brought Jim to the club. "Will that teacher, Father O'Malley be able to give me any details, do you think?"

"He might do, but he left Glasgow a few years ago, after Jim went into the army. I think he is now teaching at a private school in Perth. Maybe he could help you out. I don't know what the school is called, but it is sure to be saint something or other. You know how these catholic schools are."

Tom prepared to leave, but Tim made one further comment.

"Despite what I have said, if I had a daughter I wouldn't want her to marry Jim Doyle. I admire the progress he has made in karate, but I think he has a vicious streak that he'll not always be able to control." This comment seemed to echo some of the misgivings that Tom himself felt about Doyle, but until he knew more about his family background he didn't want to jump to any conclusions about his suitability as a husband for his sister.

Tom then made some inquiries about the school where Father O'Malley was now teaching. Tim Dexter's information had been right so Tom made a trip to Perth where he met the teacher priest on a Saturday morning. They met in a cafe in Perth, close to the railway station. Jim counted on getting enough information in a fairly short time so that he could get the train back to Edinburgh in time to watch Hearts match against Rangers at Tynecastle. When he told the priest about hoping to get to the match, Father O'Malley expressed the hope that Hearts would prevent Rangers from winning so that Celtic's position at the top of the league would be improved. From this Tom judged that the father was one of the large group of priests who were avid Celtic supporters. Father O'Malley proved to be a tall, robust man in his mid-fifties, carrying no extra weight and looking a good example of a man who did regular physical exercise.

Tom explained why he had requested a meeting. The father expressed no surprise when Tom started asking him questions about Doyle, and even seemed glad to be able to talk about him.

"That boy caught my eye as soon as he started at our school. You know how some people appear to be uptight like an over- wound spring with that appearance of lots of energy ready to burst out. Jim was just like that. I ran the rugby at that time, and I couldn't wait to get him into the squad that I had. He was a cert to play at scrum-half, if he had any ability at all with handling a ball."

"At training he used to run himself into the ground. Not like some of the others who could hardly raise a gallop. It was clear from the start that he had a knack for the game.

He could see things around him that made him able to run the game. He was such a natural that I could see him going places at rugby." "At times he got really incensed if things did not go his way, but I used to referee the lower teams matches so I could keep tabs on him, making him take it easy instead of blowing his top. After just one year I put him into the second team and things seemed to be going well. He was still very fiery and occasionally had to be reprimanded, but there came a match, which I happened to be refereeing, and things didn't go so well. He was still small for his age, and playing with boys two or three years older than him.

He could hold his own as long as the ball was swinging about but when play got tight he was getting roughed up a bit. One of the opposing forwards had obviously marked him out for some hard attention, but Jim got wise to it and went for the boy before he himself could get hurt."

"Well, I don't mind some spirited stuff in the game, but Jim went for this chap, with his fists and his feet as if he were mental. It just took a few seconds and Jim had him on the ground with blood everywhere. I didn't think it was possible for someone to do so much damage in such a short time. I had no option but to send him off and ban him from the rugby squad altogether."

Tom was shocked by what he had heard, but then asked whether the father knew anything of Doyle's background.

"Well, I made some enquiries. I wrote to his home and asked to see his parents. It turned out he was an orphan. The headmaster had known, but hadn't made it public. I met Jim's grandmother, or the woman he called Gran, and asked her about Jim's parents. She could not tell me much, just what his mother had told her. The father had apparently died before he was even born. At first Jim had lived in Ireland before he was brought to Glasgow to live with his Gran who was actually a distant relative of his mother's grandmother."

"After his mother had died just over a year previously he had just continued to live with the old lady. I told her about what Jim had done and asked of he had had any previous trouble at his lower school. She said there had been no trouble, but I didn't believe her. I checked out at his old school and found that there had been frequent occasions that he had gone almost berserk, once just before he left the school. They had thought of having him tested psychologically, but did not go ahead with it." "I'd been thinking the same thing, But I took pity on him and suggested to him that he take up other sports. He even took up Karate and joined a club with me. I thought the discipline would do him good, but after just a few months he was in trouble there. The club leader spoke to me about him and between us we got him reinstated. After that he seemed to be progressing well at karate and I didn't hear of any more trouble. I lost touch with him when I came here, but I did hear that he is doing well, got a black belt and is running his own club in Edinburgh. He isn't in trouble again, is he?"

"Not that I know of" said Tom, and then told him of his own interest in Doyle. "I'd just like to know more about him if he is going to marry my sister. Maybe I'm being stupid, but I think I have some responsibility in this. I don't want my sister to find out that she is married to someone with a family history of mental trouble. Some of the things I hear make me suspect that all is not well with that family, but I can't find any way to get the full story."

Father O`Malley apologized for not being able to give any more information, but offered his own opinion. "I am obviously used to looking for the best in people. I think that the young man I used to know has many fine qualities. If he`s now successfully working with youngsters he`ll need these qualities. To get his black belt he must have convinced his examiners that he has the moral strengths as well as the physical attributes for a high level Karate man, and I don`t think they hand black belts out willy- nilly. There has always been a vicious streak in him. Whether he is now in full control of it, I suppose only time will tell."

Tom felt that he was no further forward. He`d seen Jim in action as had the two men he had now met, men who had been witness to some of Jim`s violence. Was it still there, or had he now conquered what was an obvious flaw in his character? Where the hell could he continue his investigations? With Gran and Jim`s mother now dead, it was clear that if he were to get any more information on the Doyle background he would have to talk to the man himself, or ask Margaret to ask the questions for him. But what if Margaret and Jim were content to continue their relationship as it had been going, without any plans for marrying? Tom felt very frustrated.

He then recalled that Margaret had mentioned that Doyle`s mother had lived in Coventry. But Doyle had been born in Ireland, and Tom didn`t even know when he`d been born. He didn`t want to alert Margaret to what he was doing so had to consider any other way that was possible to get some further details.

CHAPTER 17

After a great deal of thought, Tom decided to treat his search for information about Jim's background as if he were carrying out just another search on behalf of some major industrial or commercial client. He knew that the outcome could prove costly, certainly in financial terms, and potentially in causing heartbreak, but now that he'd started on the case he was determined to chase it through to a close.

The case was proving more difficult than any that he had previously dealt with, mainly because he couldn't establish a base line from which to start. He went over in his mind the various things that he'd learned about Doyle. Realizing that Doyle's army background gave him an advantage that he had not previously considered, Tom approached a former colleague, explained what he was up to, and obtained Doyle's date of birth which gave him a start. In addition, on the promise of a future drinking session with the former colleague, Tom was promised a copy of Doyle's army records, and notes on the case in which he had interviewed him in Aldershot.

The date of birth, 6th February 1946, and the earlier casual statement from Jim about being born in Limerick, enabled Tom to approach the records office in that town to obtain a copy of Doyle's birth certificate. The mother's name was shown as Mary Doyle, and the father's name as "not known". The signature on the certificate was that of Terence Maxwell, and the qualification "grandfather".

Tom considered trying to get in touch with Mary's grandparents, but realized that as Doyle was now thirty-one, it was unlikely that they would still be alive. However, remembering other investigations he had led, he got in touch with a newspaper in Coventry, which Margaret had heard Jim talk about as his mother's birthplace. He took an advert in the local newspaper and in a Birmingham paper, asking for information about Mary Doyle, who was believed to have left Coventry in the summer of 1945. He gave a telephone number where he could be contacted. Tom had realized that it was a real stab in the dark, but was pleased to get a call within a few days, from a woman who said that she had been a neighbor of a couple called Doyle. This couple had had two daughters who had been teenagers at the time he was interested in, the older girl had left home around that date. The family had continued to live there for several years, until the younger daughter married and left Coventry, but the couple had both been killed in a road accident in the early 60's. She was unable to give any more information that might help Tom.

It was some days later that he received a more hopeful call, this time from a woman who lived in Birmingham. The woman, Shirley Malcolm, whose maiden name was Doyle, said that her sister, Mary, had left their home in Coventry at the end of the war, when she was fifteen years old. She had gone to Ireland to live with their grandparents, Mr and Mrs Maxwell, on their farm in Limerick. At the time Shirley had been twelve years old.

She remembered that after a party to celebrate VE Day her sister had been attacked and badly beaten up. It apparently affected her mentally and after a few weeks in hospital she had gone to live with her mother's grandparents in Ireland. She had never got better and had died in Ireland, after a few years, without any of her family having seen her again. Shirley's parents had been badly affected by the attack on Mary. They seldom talked about it in her presence but it was clear that they blamed themselves for what had happened.

It was clear to Tom that he could not describe the reasons for his interest in a phone call, so he asked if he could come to Birmingham to meet her. She was quite willing to do this and he arranged to visit several days later. He simply told Margaret that one of his enquiries required him to go to Birmingham. She accepted what he was saying, and he left to drive south.

Shirley lived in a detached house in Solihull, in a suburb that seemed to house many professional people, according to the size of plots, the expensive range of cars that stood outside detached garages, and the landscaped gardens that were mostly well- tended. Shirley herself appeared to be in her early forties, a self- assured woman who was apparently at ease in her surroundings. She ushered Tom into the conservatory at the rear of the house and set a coffee jug and cups on the table before she asked how she could help him with his enquiries.

"I was intrigued to see your piece in the paper about Mary Doyle. My parents were very secretive about why Mary had gone off to Ireland. I remember how Mary was after her attack. The injuries she had soon healed up but she moped about and wasn't the same person. Mum and Dad were very upset about her and they had long talks with the priest. I never knew what exactly was wrong with her. They thought I was too young to be burdened by such things."

"Up till then we had been a very happy family. We spoke about everything openly, but after the attack- I knew it was an attack and not some accident- Mary hardly uttered a word, and Mum and Dad just froze me out of their conversations. It was awful. I hated it, and I gradually began to hate my parents for the way they treated me. I stayed with them, but we were never the same again. When they told me that Mary had died in Ireland I couldn't believe it. They never once visited her, and they didn't even go to her funeral. They told me she had never recovered." "Eventually, we just drifted further and further apart. I left home when I was old enough. They didn't are what I did. Although they were at my wedding we were never friendly again. I am sure it was something to do with Mary's attack that caused the change in them. They were so miserable after it, and it felt a bit of a relief when they had the accident that killed them. I sometime wonder if it was really an accident. Dad was an expert driver and it seemed strange when the accident happened."

Tom realized that he had a difficult task ahead of him, explaining that her sister had not in fact died in Ireland, but had had a son and had gone to live in Glasgow. This would mean revealing that her parents had deceived her for many years, and he was nervous about her reaction to this news. He could not see how to break the news gently, so went right into the story that he had been constructing over the past few days.

"Thanks a lot for agreeing to talk to me. You might wish that I hadn`t come today, for what I`m going to tell you will come as a shock. I am fairly sure that your sister didn`t die in Ireland, but left there in about 1950, with her son who was born in 1946." Shirley was indeed shocked. The self-assurance was badly strained and her first reaction was, "we can`t be talking about the same person. My sister couldn't do anything like that without me knowing. We were so close, more like twins than just sisters, despite the age difference."

Tom felt awkward, having to tell her what he knew, but had to plough on with it. "I could be wrong, but let me explain. There is a young man in Edinburgh who knows nothing about his background, apart from a few snippets that his mother told him. I want to know about him for I believe he is intending to marry my sister. I`ve tried several ways to learn about him. I`ve discovered that he was born in Limerick to a Mary Doyle who at the time was living with her grandparents, Terence Maxwell and his wife."

Shirley gasped, "They`re my grandparents. I haven`t heard from them in years. How did you find them?"

Tom explained how he had obtained Jim`s birth certificate, signed by Terrence Maxwell, and showing the father to be unknown.

Shirley was still adamant about her sister. "Mary could never do that. She was the nicest person you could ever meet, would have nothing to do with boys, went to church regularly, top of her class at school. Are you sure we`re talking about the same person? I think you are talking about someone else."

"I wish I was" said Tom, "One of the things that Jim mentioned to my sister is that his mother came from a place near Coventry. Didn't you come from there? I put an advert in the Coventry paper when I did the one in Birmingham. A woman called Simpson called me. She spoke of a family called Doyle who lived near her. One of the daughters went to Ireland, the other got married, and the parents were killed in a road crash. Did you know Mrs Simpson?

"Of course" said Shirley, "she was our next-door neighbor.

But that doesn't prove anything."

"I know" said Tom, "but it would be a hell of a coincidence if there was more than one Mary Doyle, one of two sisters, and with grandparents called Maxwell who lived in Limerick, wouldn't it?"

Shirley had to accept the logic of this argument, and went on, "But what do you hope to gain from this? You'd better tell me what you know. This is all a bit of a shock to me."

"I'll tell you what I can" said Tom, "but I'm still groping about in the dark myself. This young man, who calls himself Jim Doyle reckons that he came to Glasgow from Ireland with his mother when he was about four years old. They went to live with a Mrs Wilsher, but both Jim and his mother called her Gran" "Well, that's not right for a start. My sister's grandmothers are called Maxwell and Doyle, so it can't be the same family you are talking about."

"It seems that this woman was not related, not closely anyway, but she did take Mary and Jim in. Mary died in 1958........ "Mary died in 1958?" Shirley was obviously upset at this, and Tom regretted that he had not been more careful in what he had said. So wrapped up in his own interests, he had not mentioned Mary's death before that, and realized that Shirley had probably been thinking that he had been about to tell her that her sister was still alive and well. He apologized for the way he had broken the news of Mary's death. Shirley was unable to go on for several minutes, but when he thought she had recovered her composure Tom told her what he knew.

"Jim continued to live with Gran until she died two or three years ago. They must have been very close, for the woman who he called Gran left him her rather large house in Bearsden, near Glasgow. He is now thirty-one years old. He is an expert at karate and runs his own club in Edinburgh. I believe I've found out as much as I can about his mother, but I would like to know about his father as well."

Shirley was becoming interested in what Tom had told her.

"Why don't you ask Jim himself. He must know something? "Well" said Tom, "He's very reticent on the subject. I believe from the little he has said on the subject that he's very bitter that his mother would never reveal to him just who his father is. She had told him some story about marrying a cousin called Doyle who had come to England from Ireland. Apparently they had married, but soon after the marriage he had been killed in a building site accident when a trench collapsed on him and another Irishman. When she discovered she was pregnant she had had a mental breakdown. Her parents had sent her to her grandparents to help her recover"

"That's rubbish." said Shirley, "I would have known about it if it was true. How could she lie to her son like that?"

"Well, I think Jim realizes it's not true as well. But someone has created the story, and without anyone to question it, it has been repeated many times. Jim heard exactly the same story from his Gran as well. She seemed to believe it."

"Just a minute," Shirley exclaimed. "you said that you had obtained a copy of the birth certificate. What was the date of birth? That would tell us when Mary got pregnant. And we would know where she was at that time."

"I have it here" said Tom. He brought out the copy that he had received from the Limerick registrar. "Here it is. James Doyle, born 6th February 1946."

'Right, then given a normal pregnancy Mary must have conceived him around ...... early May. Where would Mary have been then? Oh, Christ, No!".

"What's wrong?" asked Tom, seeing Shirley going pale.

"8th May 1945. Does that ring a bell with you?"

"Of course. That was VE Day"

"Exactly! The day that Mary was attacked...But it wasn't just an attack --- She was raped...How awful. ...That is what all the secrecy and hatred was about.... My parents couldn't bring themselves to admit what had happened...... They sent Mary to Ireland so that no one, including her little sister, would know that Mary had been raped, and had become pregnant...... God, the catholic church has got a lot to answer for."

Tom was amazed at the course things had taken. Shirley must have a very sharp mind to go through the logic in such short sharp steps, but of course she must be right. But he could not understand the comment about the church.

"That`s a huge jump you made. But why conclude that about the church?"

"That party she was at was in the church. It must have been one of her church friends. And the priest. He was around the house so much after it happened. I wouldn`t put it past him to make up the story for my parents about marrying, and going off to Ireland. I`ll bet he was the one who persuaded the family not to have an abortion!"

Tom could see that Shirley was now very agitated. He wished that he had not brought it about, but he could not argue against the logic of what Shirley was saying. "You might be right, but I wouldn`t go about shouting the things you have just said. It doesn`t follow that because the party was in the church, the attacker must have been known to Mary. Besides, the birth may have been premature. She would have had time to meet someone in Ireland and become pregnant, and give birth at that date. I think we should examine this carefully."

Shirley rose to make some more coffee, and on her return she seemed more composed. "You`re right, she said, "I let my mind run away there, but let`s look at it a bit more closely. I was in bed that night when Mary came home so I didn`t see her. I learned afterwards that she had been taken to hospital with bad bruising to her head, and evidently in a bad state of shock. When I visited her in hospital she looked in a dreadful state. She wouldn`t talk to me, but then she wasn`t taking to anyone." "My parents told me that she had been attacked, but no-one knew who her assailant was. I heard that the police made a lot of enquiries, but without a statement from Mary they had very little to go on. When I thought about it being a rape, I just jumped to the conclusion it must have been one of the boys at her club. I know that was a bit hasty but surely we can do something about finding out who it was?"

Tom was pleased that she had calmed down and was now thinking more clearly about what he had told her. However, he could not offer her a lot of assurance that anything further could be done about it. "It's more than thirty years since it all happened. We don't know that she was raped, and I'm not sure that the police would entertain any suggestions to have the case reopened. I have to deal a lot with the police. I used to be in the Military Police, so I could probably get them to talk to me about it, if there is still anyone there who can remember the case. Would it have been the Coventry police or Birmingham police who dealt with it?"

"Almost certainly the Coventry police" said Shirley.

"Right, I'll try to see them and find out what I can. I'll let you know how I get on with them."

With that, and after apologizing profusely for being the bearer of bad news, Tom got in his car and headed for Coventry.

Chapter 18

As he travelled the few miles to Coventry, Tom wondered about what he could say to the Coventry police. He had so little to go on, apart from the name Mary Doyle, and the date 8th May 1945. It was quite possible there would be no one around who had been there at the time, although if the police had been involved their records should still be available. In his experience, he had always found the police co-operative, so he decided just to see how thing went when he got there.

The first person to whom he spoke suggested that he should write and explain what he was looking for, giving what details he could, but Tom protested that he had come from Edinburgh to find out what he could from a source in Birmingham. Although he had established the identity of the person he was enquiring about, and the date of an incident in which she had been involved, there was little else he could include in a letter. Was it possible to talk to anyone who is still around, and maybe have a look at any reports that were made? He gave Mary's name and the date of the incident. The receptionist arranged for him to see a senior officer, and after a long wait a middle-aged, uniformed police sergeant asked him to accompany him to a meeting room.

"You're lucky" said the sergeant, "I'm the only one here who was involved in the Mary Doyle case. If you'd left it just a few months longer, I would have been pensioned off. Now, how can I help you?"

"I'm not sure you can" said Tom, "I might be on a wild-goose chase here. I am trying to establish the father of a man who was born in Ireland to a woman who went there from Coventry just after the end of the war. Apparently the mother was hurt in an attack after a VE day party. She was only fifteen or sixteen at the time, and was later sent to live with her grandparents in Limerick. It may be a coincidence, but she gave birth to a son almost precisely nine months after VE day. Is there any way I can find out if she was in fact raped in the attack, and was the man ever found?"

"Well, the only coincidence is that I was here when that incident happened. I was just a young copper, fresh as hell, and I'd never seen a young girl in such a state as Mary Doyle. The whole place was celebrating that night, and half the population must have been sozzled. We kept getting reports of drunkenness, but they were all light-hearted affairs that we were advised to ignore. But sometime during the night we were called to attend at the City Hospital where a young girl had been admitted, suffering from bruising to her head and severe shock. We learned that she had been found in a very distressed condition, lying on a pavement not far from her home. At first we put it down to too much celebrating, falling down and hitting her head and then being unable to get to her feet again."

"Her parents had brought her to the hospital. They hadn't been able to get any sense from her, but when a doctor routinely examined her it was realized that there was no question of drinking, the bruising had been caused by several blows to the head, and she was in a state of trauma. The doctor, who was a woman, had immediately suspected rape so she had carried out tests which proved that she had been sexually assaulted, very brutally, and probably several times. That is when we were called in."

"God, you've got a good memory. That was what? Thirty years ago?" Tom could not believe that it had been so easy to get that from the police.

The sergeant looked pleased at this. "Thanks, but this case has stayed with me for all those years. It was the first big case I'd been on, and I keep reminding myself about it. We weren't successful in getting anyone for it, but I had my suspicions." "What was so difficult?" asked Tom.

"Mary never recovered enough to make a statement. She was very badly affected by it and no amount of persuasion could get her to talk about it. After a few weeks her parents arranged for her to go to Ireland. If you ask me, I think they wanted her out of the way. I don't think they could stand having her around in that state. But you say she had a baby nine months later? They probably knew that she was pregnant, and couldn't stand the shame of it. They were a strange couple, Catholics, and very staunch. That would have prevented them from sanctioning an abortion."

"Well, there was also a younger sister", said Tom, "Maybe they were just trying to protect her from knowing the situation. I have spoken to her. She couldn't remember much about the actual incident, but she says that Mary never spoke to her again, and that her parents changed radically afterwards. They even told her that Mary had died in Ireland without ever recovering. No mention was ever made of a baby. In fact Mary did recover a bit physically but her mental condition was never quite right again. She suffered from severe depression for a while and died when she was about twenty-nine or thirty."

"Where did you learn all this?" asked the sergeant.

"I know the son quite well. I want to know more about him.

That's why I'm here. He is very friendly with my younger sister.

I expect to be told soon that they're going to get married but first I'd like to know just who he is. I have a business that checks out on the backgrounds of people who are being considered for executive positions with large companies. I've found out some queer things about people, and I thought I would run a check on this chap."

"But can he not help you? Surely he would answer your questions?"

"Well, that's the difficulty. His mother wouldn't tell him anything about his father. She, or her parents, had made up some cock and bull story about a teenage marriage to a distant cousin of the same name who died very shortly after the wedding, but Mary's sister Shirley knocks that story on the head. He had never even seen his own birth certificate. I got a copy of it from the registrar in Limerick. It shows the name of the father as unknown. I only learned about the VE day party from Shirley. She was shocked to hear that her sister had had a son and that she didn't die in Ireland. In fact, she and her son, Jim, moved to Glasgow when he was four years old. They lived with a distant well-off relation through marriage who was given the same story about a wedding. She is now dead so I can't ask her any questions"

The sergeant was interested in what Tom was telling him, and asked, "are you ex-police yourself?"

"No, not like you. But I was in the Military Police'" said Tom, and went on to tell the sergeant about his own background. "This sounds as if it is a long story. Instead of sitting here, what About going for a pint tonight and you can tell me how your investigations went"

'That's a good idea', said the sergeant, "By the way, I'm Fred. Most of what I tell you is not included in the record, so it's basically my own opinion of things. It might be better if we didn't discuss it here" Fred suggested a place that they could meet that evening, and gave him the name of a hotel where Tom could stay overnight.

After booking in at the hotel, Tom had a meal at a local restaurant. He actually welcomed the break before meeting Fred again for his mind was in a whirl. He could hardly believe his luck in being able to talk to one of the policemen who had attended at the hospital where Mary had been taken after her attack, and who obviously had thoughts of his own on who was responsible and on how the investigation had been carried out. Otherwise why would he have said that about what was not included in the record, and his obvious reluctance to give his own opinions in the questioning room. Tom looked forward to hearing what Fred was going to say.

Tom was quite surprised by the atmosphere in the bar they went to. There seemed to be as many women as men, the place was bright and airy and there was a large number of separate tables where couples, foursomes and small groups could sit in reasonable privacy from the rest of the drinkers. This was so different from the Edinburgh bars that he was used to, dominated by men, mostly leaning against the bar, drinking as if their lives depended upon getting as much alcohol inside themselves as possible before the closing bell rang. He reluctantly informed Fred that he found the atmosphere a lot more sociable than he had ever experience in Edinburgh pubs.

"I thought you said you were from Glasgow?" said Fred.

"No, I said that Mary Doyle and her son went to Glasgow from Ireland, but Doyle now lives in Edinburgh, like I do. He runs a karate club there."

"So he's not done too bad for himself?"

"Better than not bad. He landed lucky with the relation that he and his mother went to live with in Glasgow. When she died a couple of years ago she left him the big house that they lived in. He sold it and now owns his own gym and a flat in Edinburgh. He is also starting to do well with his club. He got his Black Belt a couple of years ago and now he is coaching full-time." "Well, good for him. I wish though it had never come about. From the evidence that I collected, his mother was one of the nicest girls around. She was well liked by everyone, including the boys that she knew. Like her parents, she was a staunch Catholic, belonging to the church youth organization and the young people's club that they ran. She had actually been at a dance there on the night she was raped."

Tom noted that Fred did not use the word "attacked" he was quite specific. When asked about it, he was quite adamant. "That girl went through hell that night. The doctor explained the injuries to her body to us. The brute who raped her had not been satisfied by a simple rape. He did other foul things to her body that beggar belief, and must have raped her at least twice. Little wonder that she went round the bend. That was not the action of a man- it was the action of a monster, a sex mad monster." "We never found out where she was raped. We assumed that she had been abducted, maybe driven somewhere, where the rape took place, and then returned to where she had been picked up. We made enquiries about any sightings of a vehicle seen parked quite close to the church where she had been. We suspected that he had driven her to some quiet place where he could do as he pleased without fear of being interrupted. Apparently she left the church at about ten o'clock, and was found well after midnight. He must have tied her up and taken his time over whatever he did. There were no marks or bruises on her back so the bastard must have set the thing up beforehand with blankets or a mattress or some such thing. It all pointed to a very well planned crime."

Tom could feel his revulsion for the rapist welling up in his throat, and then he thought of the man who might marry his daughter. The memory came back to him of Doyle saying some of his ancestors must have been real nutcases. Had he recognized something in himself that was akin to what the rapist must have experienced? The thought really upset Tom. "Didn't you have any luck in finding the man responsible?" he asked.

"We had so little to go on" said Fred. "We could find no witnesses, apart from the couple who reported the van near the church. Mary herself never said a word. We quickly established that none of the boys who had been at the dance was responsible. Besides, the whole of the city were celebrating the end of the war that night, so there was plenty of noise about the place. There would have had to be a lot of loud screaming to bring any witnesses, but it turned out that Mary's mouth had been taped up, as well as having her ankles and hands tied. Apparently the couple that found her removed the tape and the bindings." "Did you not suspect anyone then? It sounds as if it was someone who'd done something similar before that. Did you check on all the possible rapists?"

Fred seemed quite hurt that Tom had asked such a question. "Of course. We were very thorough, but every avenue we investigated brought us to a dead halt. It was pointless having suspects lined up for inspection. Mary was the only one who had seen the man, and she could not even speak. There was no description to go on, so, much as I hate to say it the case just fizzled out."

"Oh come on Fred, you said yourself that you had suspicions of your own, and implied that the records didn't contain everything. So what have you up your sleeve?"

"OK. I have been holding something back. I've not spoken about this for years, but it has always been on my mind. We had a list of possible suspects that we went through but most of them had alibis, or were cleared after long questioning, but there was one suspect that was written off because it was claimed that he had left Coventry a few days earlier. I didn't believe it. I'd gone through this man's record and he struck me as the most likely suspect. I was very young then, and my sergeant and Inspector over-ruled me when I wanted to pursue it."

"This chap was only twenty years old but had a serious criminal record which included burglary, theft from a church and sexual assault. He had been released from prison just a couple of weeks before that girl was raped. His whereabouts were unknown, and my suspicion was ridiculed by my superiors so there was no further investigation into him."

Tom had been getting steadily more emotional about the horrible experience Mary had been put through by her assailant, but also by what he considered to be the heartless reaction to the rape by her parents. Why on earth had they not sanctioned an abortion. So much despair and bitterness would have been avoided, for Mary, for Shirley and for the parents themselves.

By the time they had parted company, Tom was already regretting how much he had learned. With the knowledge that Jim Doyle had been conceived as the result of a rape, how on earth could Tom give his blessing to a marriage between Doyle and Margaret? When Margaret had told him about Doyle's anger that his mother would not reveal anything about his father, Tom had thought that Mary must have been a very harsh person. Now his opinion of Mary had changed somewhat. The kind, loving sister that Shirley had described would clearly have been trying to shield her son from what she knew. As a loving brother, could Tom now do what Mary had done, concealing the truth? If he were to disclose what he knew, he risked alienating his sister forever, but if he were to say nothing and Doyle later revealed some of the vicious traits of his father, how could Tom live with himself?

As he thought about it, Tom started to appreciate the dilemma that had faced Mary's parents in the immediate aftermath of the rape. If Shirley was right in questioning whether they had not died as the result of an accident, but in a suicide pact, could it not be that they were unable to live any longer with the knowledge of the betrayal of their daughters? What a predicament to be in.

CHAPTER 19

The third year student at Edinburgh University left her lodgings in Melville Drive at the end of her first day back from the summer vacation, ready to start her final year of studying languages. The journey from her home in Aberdeen, and the unpacking of her trunk, had left her feeling a bit down, and longing to get out to stretch her legs by having a run round Queen's Park. It was a run that she had done frequently in the previous two years and she did not envisage any difficulties. After all, as a member of the University Athletics Club, with a particular leaning towards the cross-country team, the distance would not over-tax her.

As she left her lodgings, just after five thirty in the evening she looked up to see how the weather was. The sky was a bit overcast, but she did not think it would rain. However, she reckoned that if she took her usual route of running around the Queen's Drive, in a clockwise direction, she was liable to find it getting too dark on the latter stages of her run. With this in mind, as she entered the park after passing the Commonwealth Pool, she turned to her right onto the road that encircles Arthur's Seat. If it got too dark when she got round part of the five mile circuit, she could join the bright lights on London Road to either complete her run through streets or board a bus to return to her lodgings. The mass of Salisbury Crags and Arthur's Seat looked forbidding in the gathering twilight, but she was quite confident that she could get round to the London Road end before night had drawn in.

She had been running regularly during the summer vacation, mainly around her parents' home near the beach on the North Sea, but as she progressed on the hill that would take her past Dunsapie Loch she started to think that she might have misjudged just how quickly she could get back to the more civilized part of her planned run. The long pull up the hill was tiring her legs more than she was expecting, but as she passed the loch she realized that it would take her longer to go back towards a lit up area than it would to go forward so she gritted her teeth and kept going.

The run from Dunsapie to Abbeyhill was all downhill, and with the light from London Road and the area around Meadowbank stadium to her right her misgivings about having to run in the dark faded away. The previous year there had been a rape committed on another girl student within Queen's Park, and the thought of that had been preying on Helen's mind as she ran, but as she got closer to what she considered was safety she started to mock herself for being so melodramatic. As she approached the Meadowbank entrance to the park night had drawn fully in. She was just starting to utter a sigh of relief when she noticed a male figure standing close to the park entrance. Like her, this person was wearing a track suit and running shoes, but he was clearly taller than she was. In the little light that was remaining she did notice that he had long hair and a beard.

As she tried to swerve past the man he grabbed at her arm and propelled her towards the bushes which were just within the parks boundary wall. Helen reacted quickly to try and free erself from the stranger's grasp but he was too strong. He appeared to have no difficulty in lifting her off her feet and charging into the undergrowth. She tried to scream, but he had anticipated this and had placed a hand over her mouth. The darkness prevented her from making out his features, but she had no difficulty in recognizing his harsh Glasgow accent when he told her, "ye'll only make things worse for yersel if you try tae scream." He then threw her to the ground, pulled a handkerchief from his pocket and tied it round her mouth.

There was no mistaking the strength of her attacker. She could sense the power in his arms as he was manhandling her. She could not just accept that she was about to be raped so she fought against him as strongly as she could but she was fighting a losing battle from the start. He held the upper part of her body against the ground with his right arm and lowered her track suit bottoms with the other, then as she struggled to keep his hands away from her most intimate parts he tore her flimsy pants apart. She was determined not to give in lightly to him so she beat her hands against his chest. He tried to prevent her from doing this for a few seconds, but then swung a massive punch to her right cheek with his left hand. The blow rocked her and she felt all her strength disappear as he grabbed her by the shoulders and pushed her back to the ground.

His first attempt at raping her proved unsuccessful as he could not force her legs apart because of the track-suit bottoms around her ankles. This was frustrating him, so he threw another punch to the head which effectively stopped her struggles. Helen fell back, barely conscious, leaving her attacker to pull off the bottom of her track suit, force her legs apart and then rape her. The actual rape lasted no more than a few minutes, after which he lay still on top of Helens inert body. As he lay on top of her, Helen reached behind her head and freed the makeshift gag that he had tied around her, then started to scream loudly.

The rapist's first reaction was to hit her again on the side of her head, but he quickly realized that they were not far from a road where there might be someone who could hear the screams, so he jumped to his feet, pulled up his trousers and made off quickly further into the park. He was lucky, for two young men who had been walking just a few yards away, on the other side of the park wall, came running through the entrance at which the rapist had been standing earlier. The young men did what they could for Helen, helping her to make herself respectable before escorting her to a telephone box where they made an emergency 999 call. They stayed with her, trying to console her until a police car arrived. They had made no effort to look for the assailant. It had seemed pointless. The park, all thousands of acres of it, was in total darkness and there would have been no chance of finding anyone.

The immediate reaction of the two policemen who arrived was that the two young men had been responsible for the state Helen was in, but she was able to convince them that they had in fact rescued her. She was unable to give a detailed description of the man who had attacked her, apart from saying that he was tall, bearded, very strong, and, she thought, left handed. Even in the midst of what had been happening to her, she had noticed that he had used his left hand to pull down her clothing and to tear her panties, plus the blows she had suffered were all to the right of her head.

The police made Helen's rescuers accompany them to the police station to make statements, then they were allowed to leave. Helen herself apart from the bruising to her head was feeling more humiliated and dirty than seriously hurt, but she did allow the policemen to take her to the Royal Infirmary to have a check done on her condition.

The press was informed of the incident and their news was released the following morning in the Scotsman and later in the day in the Evening News and the Evening Dispatch. The press reports were necessarily brief, but included an appeal for any possible witnesses to inform the police. They also referred to the rape case in a similar situation the previous year, and warned young female students against running on their own in Queen's Park.

Helen, a very independent young woman showed the marks of her assault on her face for several days, but they did not prevent her from attending classes, nor did she seek sympathy from any of her friends. Her mother, an equally calm reassured person, arrived as quickly as possible from Aberdeen, and although she commiserated with her daughter, they both agreed that, in the circumstances, she had been lucky to escape with her life. In another part of Edinburgh, on the morning after the rape, Jim Doyle lay in his bed wondering what on earth had possessed him to attack that young girl. He felt no remorse for what he had done, but could not believe that he had been stupid enough to abandon what he had successfully hidden from the world for years. He knew himself that some wild emotion took over his senses occasionally, but with the harsh lessons that had been instilled in him since he took up karate he had thought that he was in control of the situation at all times.

Last night he had gone out for a run, as he did several times a week before his classes were due to start. But this time some sexual urge came over him, an urge that he had been suppressing for years, and when he had spotted that young girl running down the hill towards Meadowbank he had seen the opportunity, and had grabbed it. Sex had never meant that much to him previously, in fact until last night his few sexual experiences had been with prostitutes when he had been in the army. Their purely professional approach to sex had not given him the thrill that he had been seeking, and for almost three years he had been celibate.

Last night's experience had not been planned and he took no pride in having done what he did. He wondered if he would come to regret what had happened. What if the girl were to give a good description to the police and he were to be questioned? Could he bluff his way out of trouble? Thank God, he had worn his new contact lenses last night. He had better leave them in their case for a while and wear his glasses. They won't be looking for a man with glasses. Maybe he should shave off his beard as well? No, that would expose the scars on his face and he didn't want that, but he did make up his mind to get his hair cut as soon as possible. The girl would have seen the unruly mop that he had been sporting the last few months.

Afterwards, when he had run along towards Holyrood Palace and then back to his flat, he had showered and then took his class as if nothing had happened. He felt sure that none of his pupils would be able to say that he was any different from usual. He had even gone out for coffee with Tom Mitchell after the class, and spoke about the Hibs/Hearts match that they were going to see together at Easter Road at the weekend.

The rape claimed the headlines of the local newspapers for a few days, but in the absence of witnesses and a clear description of the assailant, the police made no headway with their investigations. The victim had attended several line-ups of potential suspects in the Gayfield Square Police station where she had made her first statement, but was unable to pick out anyone who had resembled the rapist. Helen herself was determined to put the incident behind her so she threw herself into her final year's study. She developed a restrained attitude towards the male students that she had previously had relations with, which rather surprised those men, but she was not prepared to indulge in sex again while the memory of that incident remained so fresh in her memory. The policewoman who had been detailed to assist Helen in her rehabilitation was amazed at her resilience. Most girls who underwent such an experience reacted very strongly by seeking revenge, or by radical changes to their lifestyles, or some other extreme measure, but Helen concentrated on her studies and lived normally.

Jim Doyle was not even interviewed by the police regarding the rape, but he thought constantly of what he had done. He had enjoyed the whole experience. It had been thrilling to take advantage of a young woman, so much better than the prostitutes he had paid previously. The danger, and the physical blows that he had made her suffer, had made him feel that he was in charge of the situation, much as he had felt when in action in the army. The lack of any approach from the police made him feel quite impregnable, so he made plans to commit another similar offence, but this time he would choose the time and place, and even select his victim beforehand.

CHAPTER 20

One of the things that Doyle had noticed about Edinburgh was the enthusiastic manner in which its citizens took to the City Centre on New Year's eve. They turned out in their thousands to welcome in the New Year, making it almost impossible to pass along Princes Street with their bottles in hand, acclaiming the various bands and smaller entertainments along both sides of the famous street. The Edinburgh crowds were more restrained than their Glasgow counterparts, who had never lost the enthusiasm for drinking heavily the whole year round, but they still managed to enjoy themselves raucously, while retaining some kind of gentility about the entire affair.

Despite being a non-drinker, Doyle had enjoyed watching the cavorting of the mainly young crowds, feeling a bit jealous of the easy way that males and females behaved towards each other. He had never felt easy in female company, but he made up his mind that he would let his hair down on that final night of the year, as the bells pealed to welcome 1978. If he could not meet up with a girl who would welcome him, he determined that he would assault another girl.

When Hogmanay came round, Doyle had worked himself into a state of high excitement so that as he walked from his flat to Princes Street in the final hour of the year, he looked forward to a sexual encounter, mutual or otherwise. He had always been a loner, but as he worked his way through the crowds he felt even more lonely. He appeared to be the only unaccompanied person in the vast throng, watching pairs of girls and women matching up with pairs of boys and men. His awkward attempts to single out a companion for himself became more and more frantic as women rejected his efforts to join them. As the bells for New Year rang he brazenly grabbed at girls around him, in the same way as all the other, mainly well intoxicated, men were doing, but all his attempts at cuddling and kissing were rebuffed. Not for the first time in his life, he felt like an alien who stood out because of his soberness.

Becoming more and more frustrated, Doyle realized that he was going to miss out on voluntary female company again. He deliberately started to look for a pair of girls who were more inebriated than most, and quickly picked out two late teen-aged girls who were dressed less conservatively than the majority of people around. They were clearly trying to get matched up with boys. As he watched, one of them paired off with a boy of her own age, so Doyle went up to the other, took her by the arm and turned her away from her friend. "Happy New Year, Darling" he said, an expression he had never used in his life before, put his arms around her and planted a long soppy kiss on her lips. He had feared that she would push him away, but she returned his embrace, and his kiss. He deliberately continued to hug her while he watched her friend being swallowed up in the crowd so that by the time they broke apart the two girls had become well separated.

When she realized that she had lost touch with her friend, the girl became anxious, but Doyle reassured her that they would soon be together again. It was obvious that whatever she had been drinking had affected her judgment, so when Doyle offered her a drink from the bottle of champagne that he had brought with him, as part of his plan, she gratefully took a swig from it, but did not notice that Doyle himself no more than wet his lips. The girl, only slightly smaller than Doyle, then took time to examining Doyle closely. She was apparently satisfied by what she saw for she very willingly went into a clinch and started kissing him again. Doyle continued to ply her with the champagne while only pretending to drink himself, moving her further and further from where he had last seen her friend. As the first hour of the new year faded away, the crowd started to disperse but there was no sign of the girls friend. The girl appeared to be content to be hanging on to Doyle, but at one point she had explained that she and her friend had arranged to go home to West Lothian by the bus that they had hired along with several others. The bus was due to leave the west end of George Street at one o'clock. Doyle deliberately guided the girl away from the center of Princes Street towards the east end, while keeping her supplied from the champagne bottle.

He could see that the girl was by now totally drunk, and from the way she spoke about herself and her friend he gathered that she was a lot younger than the nineteen or twenty he had at first assumed. Doyle pretended to be unaware of the time, despite the large clock on the top of

North British Hotel, and the wrist watch he was wearing, until it was far too late for her to catch the bus. When he offered to take her back to his flat, she seemed to sober up a bit. It was then that she told him she was only fifteen years old, and that if he were to assault her in any way she would report him. He turned on as much charm as he could and promised that if she went back with him he would see that she was alright. He told her that he lived fairly close to Princes Street, that they could be there in a few minutes, and that he would take her to St Andrew's Square to catch the first bus home the following morning

When she reluctantly agreed, Doyle led her eastward as he claimed it was a short cut to his place, although each step took them further and further from his route home. He had known for weeks just where he would take his victim. They walked, or rather he walked and supported her as she staggered, past the entrance to St Andrew's House until they reached the entrance to Royal High School. Here, he took her behind a wall and started to take advantage of her. She had made things easy for him by wearing a short skirt that offered her no protection whatsoever, so when he pushed his hand up her skirt there was only a brief pair of pants hiding her nakedness.

Despite her age, she showed that she was sexually experienced by yielding to his clumsy groping, and by reaching towards his trousers to open the fly. Apparently what she found was a big disappointment for her because she started to laugh and ask if that was the best he could manage. Memories of the prostitute that he had encountered in Hamburg came back to him and he became very angry. He called the girl a slut for knowing about sex at her age, but that led her to telling him of some of the exploits that she had experienced with boys of her own age, all of whom put his shrivelled manhood to shame. As had happened in Germany, he lost his head, but this time he grabbed the girls throat and started to strangle her. Feeling her fighting him and making choking noises turned him on and suddenly he was quite capable of having full intercourse with her.

He pulled her knickers aside and thrust himself into her, continuing to choke her with his right hand. As he reached a climax he felt the girl go limp. He had never seen a woman have an orgasm before. He had expected it to be a noisy happening, and was shocked to realize that, instead of inducing an orgasm for her, she had died of throttling. His anger dissipated, Doyle pushed the girl away from him. Apart from the sudden release of sexual tension, Doyle felt no emotion. He felt the girls pulse and when he had confirmed that she was dead he pulled his clothes together then executed the plan that he had been hatching for some time.

He frequently ran along this road, and since the rape in Queen's Park he had noted that there was building work going on at the Royal High school building. This meant that various building materials were placed near the entrance. He now took the body of his victim, placed it alongside a large stack of building blocks then moved many of the blocks so that the body was completely hidden from sight. He knew that building sites were closed during the first working week of the year, so he counted on it being some time before the body was discovered. Having done that, he then looked around to see if he had left anything that would point the police in his direction. Once he had satisfied himself that there were no clues lying about he made his way home.

Doyle felt pleased that his plan had worked well. It was so much more satisfying than the earlier rape he had committed on the spur of the moment. He had proved to himself that he could hold his nerve and carry out a serious crime. His one disappointment was that the actual sexual experience had not been as satisfying as he had hoped it would be. Once again, he had anticipated a bigger thrill form the actual sexual climax, but like the other occasions, he had to admit that the actual administration of pain had given him more satisfaction than the short burst of his climax. There was a certain feeling within himself that he would have to accept that something within himself led to this strange craving.

He couldn't understand his lack of what he assumed to be a normal sexual appetite. For more than a year he had been seeing Tom Mitchell's sister Margaret, accompanying her to theatres and cinemas and spending much time listening to her enthusiastic descriptions of what she considered the cultural aspects of life. While he enjoyed those encounters, and indeed looked forward to them, he could not find it within himself to make any sexual advances towards her. The platonic relationship that existed between them presented no difficulties as far as he was concerned. He acknowledged that she was a very attractive woman, and that together they made a handsome couple. He was also aware of the less than subtle hints that she gave him concerning other boyfriends and her own wish to have a similar relationship with him.

He felt no jealousy about her having "real" boyfriends who could satisfy her own sexual feelings, and, as with the period over New Year, had encouraged her not to make any plans that included him.

Doyle returned to his normal routine after the New Year incident, but kept a close watch on the local newspapers to see what was reported about the girl he had murdered. There were headlines about a missing schoolgirl from West Lothian, and requests for any witnesses who might have seen her after she and her friend had become separated, but there was no indication of any progress in finding her. Stories of other missing youngsters were repeated, as were warnings about the danger of talking to strangers, but they gradually fizzled out.

It was actually three weeks into the new year before her body was found. Apparently the construction works where her body lay had been delayed due to changes in the building plans, so no one had gone near the blocks that hid the body. When it was found, it quickly became apparent that she had been raped and strangled. The newspapers once again carried banner headlines about the crime levels in Edinburgh and the need to protect the young women of the city. Once it was established that the sperm sample taken from the vagina of the murdered girl matched that taken from the student who had been raped in Queen's Park just a few weeks previously, the police came under pressure to increase their investigation. There was some surprise within the investigating team, for the escalated crime, and the vastly different circumstances did not follow any kind of pattern. To go from rape in an isolated corner of a park to what appeared to be abduction in an extremely crowded city center, followed by rape and murder was such a leap that the police were taken aback. In the absence of any response from potential witnesses from the New Year celebrations, the police had to concentrate on the description that the raped student had given of her assailant. One point that the police thought was significant was that two crimes had been committed within just over a mile of each other which suggested a local man had been involved, so they narrowed their immediate investigations. When Doyle read this in the local press, plus the description that the girl had given of him, he wondered if he was about to be visited by the police. His gym was located within a mile of the rape and about half a mile from where the body had been found- and the description that had been issued matched his own description! On top of that, the Gayfield Square Police station that was dealing with the investigation was just a matter of yards from his home. Doyle immediately reverted to wearing glasses again rather than his contact lenses, went to the hairdresser to have his hair cut short, and his beard severely trimmed. Now he could walk down Elm Row without being scared that a passing policeman might match him up to the description.

The police did in fact visit him in the course of their house-to- house interviews. If they did consider his appearance matched their description, they kept it to themselves, for he was not invited to visit the station. One person did note the similarity to the police description and made a sly comment about it to Doyle. Tom Mitchell, at the Karate class after the description had been given in the papers, casua remarked, "I suppose the police have been around to check up on you?" Doyle was taken aback and replied, a bit angrily, "Why? Do you think I did those two crimes?" Tom noted Doyle`s reaction but kept a straight face. "Don`t be daft. My place is just round the corner. I was probably one of the first people they checked on. Margaret even had to confirm where I was on the two occasions."

"God. I thought you were accusing me. They went away quite happy about me. At least they haven't come back."

Actually, Tom had been testing Doyle. For some time he had been studying Doyle, partly because of his previous suspicions about setting up the incident in Aldershot, and partly because he was becoming more aware of the relationship between Doyle and his sister. He knew Margaret was a full blooded heterosexual but suspected that the friendship between them was platonic. This didn't make sense to Tom, so he had been watching Doyle's way of dealing with the girls who were in his class. His manner was so guarded with the girls that Tom had come to suspect that Doyle might in fact be homosexual. He had no real cause to suspect this, so had tried that ploy about the police to get some kind of reaction. The reaction he got left him as puzzled as ever. Surprisingly, the police seemed to have concluded that Doyle was in the clear as regards the two crimes, and did not return.

CHAPTER 21

After more than a year of going out with Jim Doyle, Margaret was beginning to realise that she was in a no-win situation. She had enjoyed introducing him to the theatre and always found her evenings with him very pleasant, but she was looking for some advancement in their relationship from the placid platonic friendship that so often left her feeling sexually frustrated. It was not because she was living a celibate life, she had not turned her back on the various friendships she had developed before meeting Jim, and she was sure that some at least of her boyfriends rather enjoyed the way she took out her sexual frustration on them. She did not consider herself promiscuous by keeping several suitors in tow, but as she was now into her thirties, and starting to feel broody, she would prefer Jim to be the father of any children she had. But she feared that if she made the first moves, she would lose him forever

She had spoken frequently with her brother about Jim. Tom was adamant that his own relationship with Jim was more than a bit strained. Conversation was very limited, not helped by the fact that, even in pubs, Jim would never have an alcoholic drink. Neither brother nor sister were heavy drinkers, but in their sensible, civilised lives they knew that a social drink went a long way towards encouraging conversation, and the dropping of various inhibitions. Jim, though, seemed to live behind some kind of barrier.

Tom had watched Jim in class, where his pupils were both male and female, and he vowed that both sexes were dealt with in the same way. There was no closeness between teacher and any pupil. Apart from the use of first names Jim made no concession towards friendliness whatsoever. Tom knew of no one else among his fellow pupils ever having had contact with Jim outside of the gym, and Tom himself always complained to Margaret after having been out with Jim at a football match or just for a coffee, about the hard work trying to carry a conversation. Apart from the evening when they had both taken Jim out for a meal, Tom had never heard Jim reveal any personal details whatsoever.

Margaret had felt hurt when Jim had not made any arrangements to see her over the Christmas and New Year holiday period, but had determined not to let him spoil her enjoyment. For Christmas, she had gone away for a three day break with another regular boyfriend to Aviemore, where early snow had opened up the resort for skiing. She much preferred the Alps for skiing, but for the short period, the travel would have been excessive. The drive to Aviemore was no more than three hours, whatever the weather, so with an early departure on the first day, Christmas eve, they had several hours skiing, and enjoyed a fine meal in their hotel.

This friend, Alistair, a fellow worker at John Lewis's Edinburgh store was a pleasant companion who placed no pressure on their friendship. For several years they had enjoyed a sexual relationship that created no tension. No mention was ever made of marriage, and both of them understood that neither of them was under any obligation to remain celibate when they were not seeing each other. With Alistair, Margaret was able to have long conversations on many subjects, as she had done regularly since they had met at university. After the constant struggle that seemed to exist between Margaret and Jim, who would never initiate a conversation on any subject, the three days represented a welcome relief for Margaret.

On her return to Edinburgh, Margaret did not even make any attempt to see Jim. The post-Christmas sales at the store kept her on the run constantly, and each night she was glad just to stay at home resting. For New Year she went first-footing in the traditional Scottish way with a girlfriend who live fairly close to her own flat. They visited several neighbours and friends, dispensing pieces of coal at each one and enjoying the drinks that were being handed around. After calling on three or four houses, all within the vicinity, Margaret felt quite giggly and suggested to her friend that they should visit Jim's flat to be his first foot. She was sure that, being a teetotaller, he would not be venturing far from his home. When her friend protested that Jim would have gone to bed without even watching the New Year in, Margaret became even keener to go to his place and waken him up.

It was after 2am when they rolled up to Jim's flat and hammered at his door. There was no reply but Margaret continued to batter at the door for fully fifteen minutes, finally accepting that he must not be at home. Margaret then gave up and both girls returned to their homes. She felt a bit aggrieved that Jim must have gone out. When he had not asked to meet her over the holiday period, she had put it down to his non- drinking and had accepted the situation, despite having had plans for getting closer to him. Since the first time she had met Jim she had been laying plans for inducing him to have at least a glass of champagne with her and then to seduce him. She had already seen how he could relax after just one glass and the whole thing had become a self-imposed challenge to her.

After the New Year celebrations were over she became even more determined to get Jim to have sex with her, and she planned the time within the month when she was most likely to become pregnant as the time for the seduction. She had finally made up her mind to become a mother, before she was past the point where it could cause complications, and Jim was the selected father. When she spoke to her brother on this subject, Tom pooh-poohed the idea. "I am not sure that this is on. I still can`t make up my mind whether he is a homosexual or not. I`ve never seen him showing any sign of chasing any of the girls in his class, but then I`ve never seen him making any advances to any of the men either. It`s strange, but he`s the first man I`ve ever come across who has never mentioned sex. That`s strange for someone who has been in the army."

Margaret got quite cross at the idea of him being homosexual. "I have known a few men like that. You get them when you work in the clothing business, but usually I find that they`re more considerate towards women than straight guys are. But you say that he doesn`t treat the girls any differently from the boys. I think he`s just had a bad relationship with his mother.

She has put him off being friendly with anyone, not just girls." Tom then asked Margaret if she knew any details of Jim's background that he did not know. Margaret was unable to tell him very much, stressing that Jim himself never learned much from his mother about the father. Tom was a bit upset and suggested to Margaret that he should try and use his own investigative skills to find out what he could about the circumstances of Jim's birth. He said, "If you are serious enough about having this man to father your child, why don't you just marry him? But whether it is as the father of my niece or nephew, or as your husband, I want to know more about him. Can you tell me some details that will get me started?" "Well, I know that he was born on the sixth of February 1946, in Limerick. His mother told him that his great grandparents lived there and that she had gone there from Coventry when her husband had died, just after she became pregnant. They came to Scotland when he was four, and she died when he was twelve. I think she was very protective towards him, didn't like him even playing with other children, especially girls. He's been a member of some karate club in Glasgow since he was twelve or thirteen, and he was introduced to the club by a catholic priest who taught at his school. It doesn't seem very much to go on, but maybe you could make a start. Oh, he went into the army when he was twenty-three or twenty-four."

"OK." said Tom, "I'll have a look into it, but make me one promise. Don't do anything about it until I find out what I can?"

"Right," said Margaret, "but don't take too long. You know I'll be thirty-three soon. I can't wait much longer if I want to have a child. Any older and I'd never get my job back afterwards." After his visit to Coventry, Tom had begun to wonder whether he had opened a can of worms with his questioning of Jim's karate instructor, his former teacher, his mother's sister and the police sergeant. At least the chats with the sister and the police sergeant had thrown some light on the manner of Jim's conception, and explained, in some way, the reluctance of Jim's mother to disclose any details of the man who had fathered him, but Tom felt thwarted in his search for any real evidence that would entitle him to discourage marriage between Jim and Margaret.

In much the same way that he had made notes on his investigations during his military Police years, Tom started to compose a file of what he had learned about Doyle. He listed the various incidents that had been brought to his attention in one way or another: Father O'Malleys description of Jim's attack on a fellow rugby player and his account of the violent episodes at his primary school which led the teachers to consider psychiatric treatment: Jim's own admission of violent behaviour that led him to confess that he wondered about the intelligence of some of his ancestors: Tim Dexter's story of the beating handed out to two others at a karate class: the way that Jim had dealt with the argumentative football supporter at the hearts/ Celtic match: Margaret's account of how the man who had accosted her when she was out with Jim had been reduced to writhing on the ground.

Tom then recalled the first time that he had met Jim, when he had been lying in a hospital bed. This reminded him of the request he had made to his former colleague in the army, so he called him again to ask whether any progress had been made. This time he was told that something had been put together and he should receive it within a few days. His mate made it quite clear that he didn't want to talk about it on the phone.

Two days later the letter arrived, and Tom read it with interest.

"Dear Tom,

My search for some background information on Private Jim Doyle, formerly Corporal Jim Doyle, revealed a lot of interesting stuff. As you probably know, he came into the army rather later than most recruits. The Parachute Regiment usually attracts men between eighteen and twenty-one, but Doyle was twenty three when he signed up as a regular. That extra few years gave him an edge over other recruits, and he took full advantage of it. The fact that he soon let it be known that he was a bit of an expert at karate probably helped in gaining recognition as a fierce competitor and enabled him to run away with the award for outstanding recruit. Most of the men who sign-up for the Paras suffer terribly under the strict physical training that they have to endure but your man simply thrived on it.

He showed no sign of nerves at any time and responded to all his training so well that at the end of his first year he was made a lance-corporal. He did some service in Northern Ireland soon after his promotion and did so well in leading small groups that he was made up to full Corporal. He was extremely athletic, representing the regiment, successfully, in various athletic meetings, an expert marksman, but not well liked by his fellow Paras. Apparently he would never drink with his mates and held himself aloof from them.

Until he was sent to Northern Ireland on a second tour of duty he hadn`t faced any disciplinary charges, but after his arrival there he seemed to go to pieces. It seemed to have slipped the army`s notice that he is a Roman CatholiOn his first tour nothing untoward had happened but on that second tour he frequently fell out with the men under him about the treatment that was handed out to catholic youths compared to protestants. He had always had a fiery temper that he had managed to control prior to that second visit, but when the Paras became involved in what the media called `Bloody Sunday`, he apparently took exception to the way the men, for whom he was responsible, fired indiscriminately at the civilians involved.

Afterwards, he had a confrontation with the men in his squad which resulted in a set-to in the barracks. Somehow, three men were seriously injured while Doyle escaped unhurt. This was put down to his skill at karate, but he was placed on a charge and was demoted to private. When you came across him he had been sent on a fire-fighters course just outside Aldershot, where he was involved in the incident that you reported on.

The civilian police reckoned any case against Doyle wouldn`t stand up because of the attack on him. We thought we would get him on a military charge, but after what had happened in Northern Ireland his Commanding Officer was happy just to get him discharged on medical grounds. The regiment was getting a lot of flak over the Bloody Sunday affair. Apparently there were some grounds for believing that Doyle himself had fired the first shot, and the fight he had with the other three was because they threatened to reveal the true story. After the fight none of them would testify against him. The Parachute Regiment were apparently happy to see him go."

That letter gave Tom something else to think about. He was inclined to believe that Jim's action during the 'Bloody Sunday' episode arose from his concern for Catholic youths, in much the same way as he had reacted to that vile Heart supporter's anti-Catholic ranting at the Hearts/ Celtic match. However, while he could understand that impulsive reaction, he couldn't condone the vicious attack that was carried out on the perpetrator of the insults. He now began to think seriously that Jim possessed a temper that occasionally led him to wild excesses of violence.

The question of Doyle's father still stuck in Tom's mind. He had chased all the leads he could think of, except one. He had previously decided not to look up Mary's grand parents in Ireland, thinking that they would be too old to give him any information, if indeed they were still alive! However when Tom pondered the situation, he realised that if Mary had spoken to anyone about the attack she had suffered, it could have been the old couple, who had tended her during her pregnancy and in the years when she was coming out of the trauma that she had been left with. With this in mind Tom decided to make a trip to Limerick to see if he could learn anything.

CHAPTER 22

Without telling Margaret of the purpose of his trip, Tom announced that he was going to take a week's break and set off in his car. He drove to Stranraer and took the ferry to Belfast, then drove south-west to Limerick. On his arrival he made inquires about the Maxwell family who farmed within the area. He learned that there were two such families. The first farm he visited was occupied by a couple not much older than Tom himself, who informed him that they had bought the farm some fifteen years previously from a family called O`Sullivan, so he knew he was on the wrong track. He had more success at the second farm he called on.

Mr.Maxwell turned out to be a sprightly man in his nineties, obviously enjoying his retirement in the familiar surroundings of his former estate. He was very courteous towards Tom who introduced himself with the story that he had been using with others. He also described his profession and explained how he was using his investigative abilities to try and find out more about the man who might be marrying his sister. He described how he had obtained a copy of Doyle`s birth certificate and how he had found Mary`s sister. He explained that he knew about the circumstances of Mary's rape, without disclosing the police sergeant's theory about the attacker. He had no wish to upset the pleasant old man who kept filling his glass with Guiness, but had to start somewhere with his questioning. "Did you keep in touch with your granddaughter after she went to Glasgow?"

"When she left here I told her I did not want to hear from her again. Her son broke our hearts. She told me that his father was a monster, and it turned out she was right. For a young child to do what he did, he must have inherited it from his father." Jim was shocked by what he had heard. "But he was only four years old when he left here, wasn't he? What could he have done at that age to make you think that?"

The boys great grandfather became upset. Tears filled his eyes and Tom expected to be thrown out of the cottage, but the old man recovered a bit of his composure and took a long drink from his glass. "I have never spoken about this in nearly thirty years. I suppose I have been waiting for someone like you to come along and bring it up. I never even spoke about it to my wife while she was alive. She was broken hearted when I turned them away and she never really forgave me."

"What happened that night in Coventry destroyed our family and the rest of our lives. My granddaughter never recovered from it, my daughter and her husband lost their other daughter because of it, then their lives, and my wife and I were virtually parted because of it, despite continuing to live together. I can't have much longer to live so I'll tell you, but you must promise me that you'll never discuss it with anyone else."

Tom hastily gave his assurance to the old man, then listened spellbound as his story came out.

"We were shocked when we heard about the attack on Mary. We rushed to England and saw how she had become a virtual cabbage, and we argued with her parents and that stubborn parish priest of theirs about having an abortion after she found out. We were unable to get them to change their minds, so we helped them to concoct that ridiculous story about a marriage and how her mental breakdown came after the death of the fictitious father."

"We all kept the real story from our other granddaughter, and we brought Mary back to Limerick with us, hoping that we could make her change her mind about keeping the child, and not putting it up for adoption. When the boy was born we fell in love with him, and it would have broken our hearts to part with him, so we didn't press Mary any more on that subject." "At first, he was a nice little boy, but maybe because we had all spoilt him he became quite uncontrollasble at times. Mary wouldn't allow any visitors, so they lived a very sheltered life here on the farm, with him ruling over all of us. But one day, when he was four, a niece of mine visited us with her son who was about the same age as Jim. I was doing some ploughing with the tractor that day and the two boys came up to the field on the side of the hill to watch me. I was at the top of the hill and the boys were watching me from the lower part. I could see them clearly. I thought they were just playing together, but as I got closer to them I realised that they were struggling with each other, their voices raised. Suddenly I saw Jim glancing up and looking me straight in the eye then pushing the other boy. The look in his eye was pure malevolence. I tried to swing the tractor away from the boy. I missed him with the small front wheels. But the large back wheel ran right over him."

"He died immediately. There was a big to-do with the police. I didn't tell them exactly what I had seen. They accepted that it was an accident. The tractor tracks showed that I had swung it round quickly. I felt awful, but how could I explain a look that I had seen in a boy's eye. I knew, though, and that look has stayed with me for all those years. It chilled me to the bone. Afterwards I questioned Mary about the man who had fathered her child because I was scared that we had a boy with an uncontrollable temper in our house. I told her she and Jim would have to leave, that they were no longer welcome in my house."

"I felt sorry for Mary, especially when she told me, for the first time, about the boy's father, describing him as a monster, just like her son was turning out to be. I had expected her to take Jim back to her parents, but they had been having difficulty with their other daughter, who had been kept in the dark about Mary's rape and her child, so she made other arrangements. An elderly relation of my wife had died, leaving his widow a house in Glasgow, and they went to live with her. We never heard from her again, and soon after we heard that her sister had left home and her parents had been killed in a road accident. We went back to Coventry for the funeral, but Mary didn't even turn up for that. As I said, the family was destroyed by that attack on Mary."

Tom had listened, shocked, but thought he had better contribute what he knew. "Well, your great grandson is still in Scotland, but he now lives in Edinburgh, the same as me. His mother died when he was twelve."

"I knew about that," the old man said. "I said that we had never heard from Mary again, but I got a letter from her. The most tragic letter I've ever read in my life. I've never told anyone about this, not even my wife, and you mustn't tell anyone either.

I'll only tell you because of the possibility that your sister might marry my great grandson. If you have any feeling for her at all you'll make sure that such a marriage doesn't take place." Tom wondered what on earth he was going to hear, and even whether he should hear it. However, he assured the old man that he would not reveal anything about the letter, but kept his fingers crossed that he was not committing himself to an impossible promise. Mr. Maxwell rose, went to an old bureau that stood in the corner, and extracted a letter from a document folder. He opened the envelope and showed Tom a hand- written letter and a folded newspaper cutting. Tom took the letter. It was clearly written, if a bit spidery, but Tom immediately grasped the import of it.

He read, *"Dear Grandad, I've kept faith with you, never written in all the years I've been here, long miserable years with only cheery Gran Wilsher for company. After we got here I soon found how bad my son was when he was involved in the death of yet another young boy. She has been repeatedly punished for his uncontrollable behaviour. I couldn't take it and had Gran Wilsher deal with teachers. She has never given up on Jim, defending him faithfully. She will soon find out just how bad he is.*

I've kept up the lies that we invented, especially for Jim, but recently he's been nagging me for some details of his father. How could I tell him that his father was a rapist.

I have never forgotten that night. it lives with me constantly. Each time Jim asks me about his father it comes back as if it was yesterday. Then today we were arguing again. He threatened to strike me and I called him a monster, just like his father. When he threatened me he stuck his face close to mine and it was like looking into the eyes of that monster. Jim stormed out of the house and now I will never see him again. Just after he left I noticed a headline in the local newspaper and the picture of a man who had been hung for murder and rape. I had only caught a quick glimpse of the man who raped me but this picture reminded me of him. Do you think all rapists have piercing black eyes and aquiline nose?

But I will never have to look into those eyes again. I knew this day would arrive. I've been keeping a lot of the tablets the doctor has prescribed for me, and now I'm going to take them all. Please pray for forgiveness for me. I've borne this cross for many years now, but it will soon be all over. I am enclosing newspaper cutting. Does the face look familiar? Your loving granddaughter, Mary

Tom opened the cutting and found a picture of the mass murderer and rapist, Peter Manuel, who had been hung in Barlinnie Prison that morning, with a brief summary of the crimes that he had committed and stated he had spent several years of his life in and around Coventry, leaving there around the end of World War II.

Tom was overwhelmed by what he had read. He couldn't prevent himself from shedding tears as he commiserated with the old man beside him. Mr. Maxwell pointed out the postmark on the envelope. It was the same date as the paper was issued, 11th July 1958. "She must have sealed the envelope, then gone out to post it before taking the pills and lying down on her bed," he said. "No one else has seen that. I didn't see any point in making it public. I think it was just her way of telling me that I was right about Jim."

Following his meeting with Mr. Maxwell, Tom returned to his hotel in Limerick, racked by strong emotions. In a way, he was sorry that he had even started to ask questions about Jim Doyle's background. The repercussions of his father's attack on Mary, were so disproportionate to the brief sexual thrill that he had experienced, that Tom wanted to inform the whole world about it. But how could he? What could anyone gain from it now? And what damage could it do to his relationship with his own sister if he were to reveal even part of what he had learned?

Tom thought of the unhappiness his quest had already brought to Mary Doyle's sister, and her grandfather, and felt guilty at having reopened their long slumbering memories. He did not doubt that there had already been sleepless nights because of him, and now he himself would have to face up to the things that he had learned. He thought of the theory that had been expounded by the police sergeant, and had to admit, in the light of what he had read in Mary's letter, that the theory was a lot closer to the truth than he had given it credit for. But did that mean that Jim Doyle had the same psychopathic tendencies that his father had had?

As he thought that, Tom realized that he was assuming that Mary had been right in her recognition of Manuel's photograph in the Glasgow newspaper. He found it difficult not to believe Mary's revelation. In the mental state she had been in for the years after her rape she must have carried the image of that man's face clearly in her mind, and it would shock no one to find it was the sight of that photograph that finally sent her over the edge. That it had happened at a time when her own son was pressing her for some kind of statement about the man who had fathered him only made Tom more convinced.

Tom had already started to build up a picture of Mary in his own mind from what he had heard from her sister, her grandfather, the Coventry policeman and the few snippets Doyle had told Margaret. He could appreciate some of her background, for he himself had been just a year or two younger than her. He had been born, just like her, into a poor family, and had suffered the privations of a life when rations and threats of bombs were facts of life. She had clearly been clever, outgoing, and of a very strong character. Even in the months after her rape she had stood up to the arguments of her parents and her priest so that she could be responsible for the upbringing of her child. When rejected from her grandparent's home, she had accepted the lonely life that she faced as a single parent, only yielding control of her son when she found out how uncontrollable he was. Even then, she had enough love for him not to burden him with the true story of his conception. It was apparently on the very evening that he tried her patience beyond endurance that she described him to his face as a monster. It took that, and the sight of that newspaper, to finally break her spirit. Tom even had a slight pang of regret that he had not met that woman when they were both young.

CHAPTER 23

On his return from Ireland, Tom was surprised to find Margaret in the flat with Doyle. It was the first time he had ever seen Doyle there. Doyle looked very relaxed and Tom suspected that it was not his first visit. The relationship between Doyle and Margaret also looked a lot more intimate than it had been and Tom knew immediately that they had become lovers. Doyle even welcomed Tom as if he some proprietorial rights, inviting Tom to sit down while he brought him a drink. Tom was completely taken aback by the situation.

There was some small talk between the three of them, initiated by Doyle, which also surprised Tom, but at least gave him time to recover his composure. He took care not to disclose that he had been to Limerick. He suspected that Doyle would have immediately associated his trip with himself, and Tom did not want that subject to come up, particularly after what he had learned.

It was Margaret who broke away from the chatter, stood beside Doyle, took his hand and then announced that she and Doyle were going to become engaged. Tom was astonished, and not a little angry, but hoped that the two of them would take his expression as being one of surprise. He quickly assessed that this was no time to act churlishly, despite the feeling of revulsion that flooded through him, so he embraced his sister, expressed his surprise, and then shook Doyle's hand, making some inane remarks about him getting a lovely and capable fiancee.

The surprises didn't stop there, for Margaret produced a bottle of champagne to toast their coming engagement and her lover- Tom had no doubt about that now- took a glass along with the brother and sister. After having been away for just over a week, Tom wondered what had caused the sudden change in circumstances, but didn't want to push it right then. It was only after Doyle left that Tom raised the subject with Margaret. "What on earth brought all that about? It's just ten days since you spoke about your relationship with that man, and suddenly you're going to get engaged to him. From the way you were snuggling up to him, I assume that you have now gone the whole way with him. I wish I could understand how your mind works!" Margaret was all bubbly enthusiasm. "Everything has changed, and I can tell you that there is no way that he is a homosexual. Just after you left he rang me. Usually I have to ring him, and then only when I've booked tickets for some show or other, but this time he really surprised me, He told me he had bought tickets for a play that I had known was coming to Edinburgh. I probably mentioned it to him at some time or another. He made bookings for Saint Valentine's Day, which was last Thursday. I'd never even thought that he would recognize the expression Valentine's Day. He had also booked a table for dinner at the Waverley hotel. I couldn't turn him down!"

"When I met him he had on a new suit that I had helped him to get from the shop, he'd trimmed his beard and his hair, and he had put on some cologne, an expensive one at that. He was really charming. Not at all the quiet taciturn man that I've told you about so often. He told me that he had decided to change his style. It was his thirty-first birthday just a few days previously, and he had apparently decided to splash out a bit. He had even read the reviews about the play, and the actors in it, so that for a change he was able to tell me all about it. I was completely taken aback, and when he ordered a bottle of champagne with dinner, that just about clinched it."

"You could not guess how much he has changed. I thought that he was bound to make a pass at me and I was wondering how I would deal with it, but he just brought me home, pecked my cheek, said how much he had enjoyed the evening and then left. I was surprised, but not too disappointed, for he asked if he could see me the next night. I met him after his class was finished. We actually went for a drink, an alcoholic drink! I thought about you as we both had a gin and tonic. I knew you would be surprised when I told you about it."

Tom grabbed the chance to say something. "Surprised? I'm amazed. But I assume you then went back to his flat with him?" "Yes, I did, but I didn't stay the night. I had no intention of getting so close to him, that quickly, but I have spent one night with him since then. He's a strange man. So shy, he wouldn't let me undress in front of him, and it was painful to see a man of his age so nervous. I don't think it was his first time, but he clearly hasn't been with many girls. I think he definitely has a mother complex, but he never mentioned her. She must have had an overwhelming effect on him."

Tom had been dying to tell his sister what he had learned, but he realized that the time for revealing anything about Mary Doyle had just slipped past. How on earth could he tell her about how the man she had now committed herself to, had been conceived, and about the identity of the father?

Tom returned to his office to find work stacked up for him. He didn't mind this for it took his thoughts away from his sister and her fiancee. For a couple of weeks the subject hardly came up between the two of them. Plans were being prepared for a party to celebrate the forthcoming engagement, but Tom was taking no part in the preparations. He was continuing to attend Doyle's classes whenever work permitted, and he watched Doyle's behaviour towards his students very carefully. To the girls, he acted in much the same way as he always did, but Tom got the distinct impression that he was acting in a more "all boys together" way towards the men, with frequent hints of new, or renewed?, sexual activity. Tom remembered the statements that from Doyle's companions in Aldershot about his aloofness, and wondered if the new Doyle was just a papier-mache figure. It was hard to believe that such a cold unfriendly person could change so quickly. Maybe it was just for Tom's, and ultimately Margaret's, benefit that the new personality was being displayed? Tom was reserving judgment on this.

The engagement party was arranged for the Saturday of Easter weekend. Margaret and Doyle had been preparing a list of people to invite. Margaret had a large number of friends, but Doyle's list was confined to a few of his Karate pupils from the class. Tom attended, and some students from the university Karate club that Doyle also ran. This surprised Margaret. She thought he would have invited some friends from Glasgow, or from his army days, but she accepted Doyle's statement about wanting to turn his back on the past and concentrate on their future together.

In all, about fifty people were at the party, held in a small hall behind a pub not far from Doyle's gym. The party-goers were from many walks of life. Margaret's friends included former classmates with whom she had kept in touch, fellow employees at her shop, and at least three ex-boyfriends to whom she was showing off her latest capture. Doyle's friends, maybe acquaintances would be a more appropriate term, included a couple of policemen, several tradesmen and students from a variety of university departments.

Despite Doyle's professed major character change, he appeared very ill at ease, as if he considered himself in a foreign environment. It was clear to Tom that Doyle was keeping away from any drink and was trying very hard to avoid the females, but this was very difficult when Margaret's friends were trying hard to find out what kind of man their friend was becoming engaged to. Several of them, like Margaret, were unmarried, independent, but sophisticated, and when they found themselves being rebuffed by Doyle when they tried to flirt mildly with him, quickly assessed that Margaret was making a mistake. They could appreciate Doyle's physical attraction, indeed his still muscular physique was receiving plenty admiration, but his painfully shy manner in conversation didn't appeal to the girls.

Doyle spent much of his time watching that the ex-boyfriends didn't commandeer Margaret's attention. It had dawned on him that when Margaret spoke of them as boyfriends, she was not just talking about boys who, like himself, had been content to visit theatres and cinemas with her, but had enjoyed sexual relationships with them. Even before the party, and for the first time in his life, Doyle was experiencing jealousy. He had even got round to thinking that some of the relationships had been continuing while he had been escorting her during the past year, and might even still be carrying on. He watched closely and it was quite evident that they were all at ease when in Margaret's company. Their conversation seemed to be light hearted, without any of the stiffness he himself had always felt, and to be truthful, still felt, with all girls, including Margaret. Apart from the conversation, Doyle could recognize the intimacy of the looks and the touches.

Tom had watched Doyle closely the whole evening. He noted the reactions when Margaret was talking to others, and he decided to stay close to Doyle for he suspected that there would be some unpleasantness before the night was over. He wasn't wrong in his judgment, for one of Doyle's pupils, a chap in his early twenties called Andrew, was showing signs of becoming drunk and had been pestering Margaret and some of her friends on and off for some time. Margaret herself was taking it in friendly fashion, but it was evident that Doyle was smouldering, ready for a fight. Andrew was one of Doyle's favoured pupils, already established on the belt ladder in Karate but obviously upset by his inability to attract the undivided attention of any of the girls. Doyle must have been aware of the situation, for as Andrew left the hall to go off to the gent's, he challenged the young man. Voices were raised, and Andrew made the mistake of pushing Doyle aside.

The younger man must have lost all reason with the amount he had had to drink for he seemed to ignore Doyle's mastery of Karate and swung some misdirected blows at Doyle's head. Doyle easily avoided the blows. He could have just eased the other man away, but instead he caught him by the hand and forearm, pulled the arm behind his back, and jerked it violently towards the side and upwards towards the other shoulder.

Andrew let out a loud squeal of pain and clutched at his shoulder. Doyle actually changed his stance and his grip on Andrew as if he was going to hand out further punishment, but Tom, who had been watching the whole incident, stepped in to part them. He had quickly realized that Doyle had at least dislocated Andrew's shoulder, and might even have caused further damage. He could see the look in Doyle's eyes. He looked completely out of control and intent on dealing out some more pain.

Doyle shot a look of intense dislike at Tom, but let him take the younger man's arm and lead him away from the hall.

Andrew was clearly in great pain and raised no objections when Tom hailed a taxi and gave the destination as Edinburgh Royal Infirmary. Tom and Andrew had a long wait at the hospital before a doctor could see the young man, during which time Tom had to keep reassuring Andrew that it was probably only a dislocated shoulder, which should be fairly simple to replaced. However when the doctor returned to Tom, he explained that it was not just a dislocation. The muscles around the shoulder had been torn, and Andrew would be in pain for a long time, with his right arm out of commission. The doctor enquired about how the injury had been sustained, and on hearing Tom's account of the incident, gave his opinion that a report would have to be made to the police as it was quite evident that that the injury was more than could have been expected from a simple affray. He tried to describe the amount of force that would have been necessary to produce that result, and expressed his own opinion that it would need to have been applied deliberately, by a person who knew exactly what he was doing.

The doctor accepted Tom's argument that it should be left up to Andrew to decide whether the police should be involved. Tom left Andrew, who would be retained in hospital for several days, and returned to the party venue. However the delay in having treatment had been so long that the place was deserted.

When he arrived back at his flat he discovered that Margaret must be spending the night with Doyle, so he was left on his own to consider the implications of what had happened. He remembered the look in Doyle's eyes as he had stepped between the two men, and he was convinced that the doctor's opinion about excessive force being used was correct. He was also sure that if he had not stepped in then the young man would have been hurt even more.

Tom wondered if anyone else in the hall had been aware of what had happened. As far as he could remember there was no one else near them as Doyle had already started to lead the young man out of the place before the pushing started. He would have liked to talk to Margaret about it, but now he'd have to wait until the following day before he could do that. If Andrew were to make a complaint to the police, Tom wondered what he himself would say if required to make a statement. The best thing would be if one or other of the two policemen at the party had been close enough to witness what had happened. Being the sole witness to the incident didn't appeal to Tom.

CHAPTER 24

When Margaret returned home the following morning she asked why he had left the party. Clearly, she had not seen what had happened, and Doyle had not explained fully. He had told Margaret that Tom had left with Andrew after the younger man had fallen against the wall and injured his shoulder. She was shocked when Tom told her that the injury was in fact serious and that he had been delayed at the hospital until after midnight, and that Andrew had been retained. He told her no more than that, thinking it prudent to wait until he had visited Andrew at the hospital, and had got a report on the extent of the injury. He also wanted to know whether Andrew was going to go to the police over it.

Andrew looked pale as he lay in bed, but managed a bit of a smile when Tom arrived. "Thank God you were there last night" he said, "you probably saved me from being even worse off than I am now. I must have been mad to try and wrestle with a fucking Black Belt. But the bastard didn`t need to do this to me.

I am going to be off work for weeks now."

Tom asked if he would get paid when he was off work

"Not a chance", said Andrew, "I'm a bricklayer. Builders don't pay you unless you've been hurt in an industrial accident, and this was no accident. But the doctor told me I should report this to the police. What do you think?"

This put Tom on the spot, right where he didn't want to be. "It's up to you, but I think you should do a lot of hard thinking before you decide. You know how courts are. They can take a long time to sort things out, and Doyle would have to be found guilty of something before you got anything out of it. Why don't you suggest to him that he should pay your wages while you're off work?"

"I don't know if that would work", said Andrew, "What about you suggesting it? You're the only one who knows what happened. You could maybe say that if it had not been for you he would have been in very serious trouble. Did you see the look in the mad bastard's eye. He would willingly have fucking killed me."

Tom was pleased that Andrew had seen the same expression on Doyle's face as he had. Maybe his opinion of Doyle, as a cunning sadist, was not so far off the mark. "Right, I will talk to him. It had better be soon, for if there is a delay, the police will wonder why it wasn't reported right away, then we'll be in the shit, so will the doctor. Maybe you should just report him. But I'll be talking to him anyway so I'll tell you how it goes." Tom called Doyle when he got back to his flat. On his way back he thought about how he would handle this, and decided that he should get Doyle to come to the flat so that Margaret could hear their conversation. Maybe it would serve in driving a wedge between the couple, which would please Tom enormously.

Doyle himself had spent a very restless night after Margaret had fallen asleep. Despite the occasion, to celebrate their engagement, neither of them had found their lovemaking particularly satisfying, but for different reasons. As on other occasions, Doyle's dissatisfaction was because of Margaret's tendency to take control of these occasions, orchestrating each move that they made. To a man who liked to be in control himself, this was humiliating. Margaret, however had over indulged in the champagne she had shared with her girlfriends, and had felt under the weather.

Doyle realized he had gone too far in his argument with Andrew, and had lain awake for a long time wondering if there would be any reaction. He hadn't realized that Tom had been watching him so closely during the evening, and had been very close at hand when the young chap had been hurt. He had even taken charge of the situation, separating the two of them, then taking the victim to hospital. Doyle knew he had overstepped the mark by dealing so severely with Andrew, but it was the culmination of increasing jealousy and realization of his own inadequacies in the company of intelligent, gregarious men and women. He recalled the comment that Tom had made to him when he had been in hospital in Aldershot. Tom had had suspicions that it was Doyle who had set up the situation when the Englishman had been killed, It was quite possible that he would have the same thoughts about this latest incident. The move that Doyle had made against Andrew was fairly well known among the higher qualified Karate men, a move that could leave a man disabled for a long time. If he had carried out such a move in competition, and gone through with it, he would have been barred from any further competitions.

Apart from that, following several weeks of sex with Margaret, which had started off so blissfully, he had come round to the conclusion that straightforward sex with a woman who wanted to dominate every procedure didn't satisfy him. He much preferred the thrill he had experienced when he had been in charge, and had been physically causing pain while experiencing a climax, as he had done with the girl in the park and the schoolgirl at New Year. Some of his sleepless time that night had been spent in laying plans for his next sexual adventure. Next time, he meant to create a different set of circumstances where his victim would have plenty of time to appreciate that she was in danger and would put up a struggle that would inevitably lead to physical punishment, and subsequently her death.

He didn't believe very strongly that his engagement to Margaret would lead to marriage. His change of character earlier had been deliberately contrived to get Margaret into his bed, but now that this ploy had succeeded he would not be particularly concerned when the match was broken off. He suspected that in a married situation he would find it difficult to indulge in any adventure that required careful planning and strange departures from home. He would work out a plan for his next escapade over the next few weeks. With this decision made. Doyle had fallen into a dreamless sleep.

He spent several hours on the Sunday in the gym, carefully honing his exercises to perfection in readiness for his next grade examination. He wondered if he would be faulted again, as he had last time round, because of his attitude. His mentor, Tim, had been telling him for years that he must at least give the impression of personal control as well as mastery of the physical exercises that he performed so well. Doyle was perfectly aware of his shortcoming, but was not prepared to demean himself even to those with superior grades to himself, or even to go through the pantomime of pretending to. To him, mastery of the physical outweighed the control of the spiritual.

CHAPTER 25

When Tom called to suggest that he come round to the flat in Montgomery Street, Doyle was taken aback. He could sense that Tom wanted to talk about what had happened at the party, whereas he himself would prefer just to put it out of his mind. However, he reluctantly agreed, and they arranged a meeting for early evening.

Doyle looked distinctly uneasy when he arrived at the flat. Tom opened the door to him and merely waved him in. He had hardly put his foot inside the door when he was nearly knocked over by Margaret rushing forward to give him a hug. Tom however, made no effort to make him feel comfortable or welcome. Margaret immediately sensed the coolness between them and went off to the kitchen to prepare coffee for the three of them. Neither of the men was willing to open the conversation, so stood silently for what seemed ages, but was probably less than a minute, before Tom ventured the first words. "Well, you fucked up my night for me and you put a decent young man in hospital with your hard man performance. Aren't Black Belt Karate men supposed to control their aggressive instincts? What you did that night was entirely out of order. You won`t be able to look your class in the eye after this if Andrew or I tell them how you behaved, You are supposed to be teaching them moderation!" Doyle was not about to go on the defensive. "You saw the way he went for me! I was just pushing him off. He can`t have been hurt badly." "Not hurt badly?" exclaimed Tom. You nearly tore his arm off.

He won`t be working for weeks. If I hadn`t stopped you, I shudder to think what you would have done to him. I spoke to the doctor at the Infirmary. He was so upset when he saw the damage to Andrew`s shoulder, he wanted to report it to the police right away. He could see that it was no accident."

That shook Doyle. "Christ, did you stop him? It would ruin my gym if he went to them. But you wouldn`t be a witness if the police got involved, would you?"

"Don`t fucking kid yourself about that" said Tom. "Remember that I also know about the chap that got killed in Aldershot, just because you didn`t hold back when you struck back at him. Yes, if it goes to court, I would be a witness on Andrew`s behalf.

What you did was away over the top."

Margaret came into the room just then. She must have heard the end of what Tom was saying, for she asked "What was over the top? You were both shouting. What is it?"

Tom immediately put Doyle on the spot. "Ask your fiance. He was closer to it than I was."

"Closer to what? I don't know what you are talking about" said Margaret.

Tom left Doyle to explain to Margaret. "It`s that chap who fell against the wall last night. Tom says he`s hurt more than I thought. He's even suggesting that I did something to Andrew. All I did was tell him off for annoying you and some of the other girls. He must have had too much to drink for he attacked me and I pushed him against the wall. I can't see how it would have hurt that much. I thought he might have dislocated his shoulder.

It's no big thing."

"We'll see how big a thing it was when the doctor describes to the police just how bad the injury is" said Tom.

"The police?" screamed Margaret. "How the hell would they become involved?"

Tom didn't hold back on what he had to say. "Andy is lying in a hospital bed with all the muscles in his shoulder torn. Your fiance almost tore his arm off. The doctor who treated him is so appalled that he wants to report the injury to the police. I asked the doctor to leave it up to Andrew whether to call the police or not. Personally my advice would have been to make the report, but Andrew's worried about the loss of wages for the next few weeks. He wants me to talk to your fiance here to get him to agree that he would make up for any wages he loses. If he does, Andrew will not press charges."

"You didn't tell me that" shouted Doyle. "Why didn't you say anything about that?"

Tom was seething. It was as if Doyle was accusing him of something underhand. "I haven't had a chance to tell you, you were too busy making out that nothing had happened, or if it did then it was slight. We both know it was your fault, but I haven't heard a word of regret from you, just trying to slide out of it." "Well, of course I regret it" said Doyle, "nobody likes to see someone get hurt."

"You should have thought about that before you attacked that young man the way you did. Isn't that the whole essence of your sport?" Tom knew that he had Doyle at a disadvantage and he wanted to see him squirm.

"Oh, come on, Tom" said Margaret. "You seem to be implying that Jim did it deliberately, and wanted to hurt Andrew as much as possible. That can't be true. Why did no one else see what was happening? You must have got it all wrong. Look, if Jim had done it deliberately he could have killed Andrew. Is that not what Karate is all about. Responding to an attack by disabling your opponent?"

"No" said Tom. "In fact it's the very opposite. It's about acquiring the skills to disable an opponent in a given situation but also learning the personal control not to deliver the actual blow. A Black Belt especially should never have carried out such a move for his own personal gratification. Your fiance could have disabled Andrew by any number of simple holds, but he deliberately chose one that destroys muscles." Tom was continuing to use the phrase "your fiance" instead of using Doyle's first name, not just because the name stuck in his throat, but also to make Doyle feel more disturbed and aggressive. If he could expose to Margaret just how out of control Doyle could become, he thought that she might see through him.

Instead, Margaret seemed to take the role of negotiator in the situation. "Come on. You're both grown men, there's no need to have an argument about it. Let's talk this through. I'm sure neither of you want Jim to be in trouble with the police. That would do nobody any good." She turned to Tom. "Tell us what Andrew was suggesting. If we could come up with some arrangement then the whole thing would be dropped."

It was Doyle who reacted to this first. "No way. I am not going to be blackmailed into paying him for not telling the police about a slight accident that left him unable to work for a while." "Fair enough" said Tom. "I`ll tell Andrew that. But I think you are being foolish. If this goes to the court you`ll get the doctor telling about the extent of the damage caused by your `slight accident` and I`ll be telling them what I witnessed. And I am not going to lie on your behalf. My sympathy lies entirely with Andrew. No one will ever believe that it was an accident. The doctor reckons that it would take an extraordinary leverage against the shoulder to produce that result, and there can`t be many men in Edinburgh capable of doing such a move. I don`t think you`ve got a chance of getting away with it. Besides, think of what it could cost you if you were found guilty. Would it be worth it?"

It was Margaret who came back on that one. "What are we talking about here? He wouldn`t be asking for a million, would he?"

"Of course not. Andrew`s not an unreasonable man. I think he just wants to be assured that he wouldn`t be out of pocket by not being able to work. He is aware that he may have been a bit drunk, and gave the first push, but doesn`t think that justified what Jim did to him. I don`t know how much he earns, but if we all agree I think Jim and Andy should meet to discuss it." Tom had deliberately used Doyle`s first name this time. He could feel the tension easing a bit and thought that, by using his first name, Doyle`s attitude might soften.

Aparently it worked, for Doyle took a less aggressive line. "Well, you talk to Andrew. Or bring him to the gym one night and we`ll see if we can come to some arrangement."

"I don't think that would work" said Tom. "It would be better if I could go back to him with an assurance that you would make his wages up to what he usually gets. It has to be decided now for the police won't like it if Andrew leaves it a while before reporting it. Can I go back and tell him that?"

Doyle thought about it for a couple of minutes, obviously weighing up the odds in his mind, then accepted Tom's proposal.

"Right" said Tom, "I've got Margaret as a witness. You'll ensure that Andrew won't be out of pocket because of what happened, if he doesn't prefer charges against you?"

"OK" said Doyle. "I'll witness that" said Margaret.

Margaret and Doyle then left to go to the cinema, leaving Tom to ponder on what he had just done. It would probably please Andrew when he was told of how the situation had been resolved, but Tom himself felt tainted. His instinct had been to see Doyle receiving as much punishment as possible for what he had done, even to the extent of seeing him lose his livelihood as a Karate trainer. He had never been enamoured of Doyle, and suspected, more than ever now, that he was capable of hurting a lot more people before he was finished.

CHAPTER 26

Andrew thanked Tom for getting Doyle to agree to pay him while he was off work. It settled his mind a bit, especially as he would not have liked to be questioned about how drunk he had been at the engagement party, or how he had quite uncharacteristically upset one of Margaret's friends. He was unused to drink and realised that he had been beyond the stage where he would be acting sensibly. To have tried to fight against a black belt was sufficient proof of his condition that night. He regretted the fight and the outcome, for he could not see himself returning to the karate classes after he recovered. He had enjoyed the classes, but now they were to be a thing of the past. Tom thought seriously about giving up Doyle's classes as well. He thought it would be embarrassing to go back after the things he had said to Doyle, but then decided to stay with them. His original thoughts about Doyle were proving correct. The man was cunning, setting up situations where he could get some kind of satisfaction from having a physical confrontation with others, knowing his superior fitness and technical knowledge of karate gave him a huge advantage. The best way for Tom to find out anything further about Doyle seemed to be to stay in his class, and occasionally meet him in closer circumstances.

In the past, he had seen a lot of Doyle, sometimes going to football matches with him, staying after classes to have coffee, and on the odd occasion having a run with him over some of Tom's own favourite circuits. Although Doyle had been a good track athlete in his youth, he preferred to take runs at different times of day around the streets and parks of Edinburgh and Leith. In their early days together Tom had shown Doyle runs of various lengths, some of which kept close to bus routes when the weather was bad, some around parks which were normally deserted, and others where there were great views to be seen. Tom and Doyle lived within a few hundred yards of each other, in a part of the city that gave immediate access to many such runs.

After the engagement party, Tom kept away from Doyle, apart from the time they met in the karate class, hardly speaking to him, but still hearing things about him from Margaret. She was disappointed the Doyle's new personna did not last very long, and she complained continuously to Tom that Doyle had reverted to the same person he had been previously, or maybe worse. Now she seemed to detect some sinister aspect in his silences, and found his increasing inclination to drink disturbing. In her own words to Tom, she thought "He seems like a smoldering time bomb, waiting to go off. He was always a bit like that, but it seemed to make him attractive before, now he can be quite repulsive." Tom did not mind hearing that, for he would still prefer that Margaret part company with Doyle, and now it seemed a distinct possibility.

Doyle himself realized that things had changed. Although engaged, Margaret and he seldom discussed wedding plans. When they had sex together he made it plain to Margaret that he disliked her taking charge of proceedings. Margaret accepted that situation, and tried to tell Doyle that she had seen the initial lack of sexual experience in him and had merely tried to let him know that the best sex did not arise from having the male dominate the scene. She still enjoyed their sex sessions. Doyle was so strong and virile that his lack of size never impaired her enjoyment, although she suspected that it disturbed him that he was less well-endowed there than in the more developed parts of his superb physique.

When Doyle thought about sex, it was with a feeling of disappointment. He had thought that becoming Margaret's lover would bring continuous sexual thrills, but in retrospect he realized that the best sexual experiences he had had were with the girl he had raped and the one he had strangled. Within a couple of months of their engagement party Doyle had begun to think seriously of committing a further attack on a girl, and on those nights when he lay in bed on his own he thought about how he could plan it. He was aware of the prostitutes that were available in Edinburgh, as in any city. His home was within half a mile of Rose Street, the long-standing centre of prostitution in the city. He had frequented the pubs along that thoroughfare on many occasions, but was more repelled than attracted to the whores who plied their trade there.

Often, after leaving Rose Street he would wander through Waverley Station and noted the young girls who arrived by the London train. Invariably the last train in each night seemed to bring several girls who were carrying bags or suitcases which gave him the impression that they had arrived from some distance away, with the intention of staying for some time. He determined to plan on picking up such a girl and then taking advantage of her.

On a warm, clear summer evening in late June Doyle had completed his plan. When he left home he was wearing a track suit and plimsolls, but had a back pack that contained a suit, shirt and tie, and shoes. As he left, he knocked at his neighbour's door. He told the old woman that he was going out running, and would be going to the all-night laundry, hence the bag on his back. He was expecting his fiancee to call later. If she heard Margaret, would she tell her that he would ring her later. The neighbour agreed to this.

Doyle set off for Waverley station. He went directly to the Gent's toilet where he locked himself in one of the cubicles while he changed into his suit. He placed the track suit and the plimsolls in the back pack, walked out to the station and placed the bag in a left-luggage locker.

He then purchased a platform ticket at the station, went onto the platform where the London train was due and watched carefully. He noted a girl who was not exceptionally well dressed and who carried a case which had seen better days. He joined in behind the arriving passengers some yards behind the girl. As they passed through the gate, after yielding their tickets he speeded up a bit, bumped into her case and then knocked her over. He contrived to trip over the case himself and landed on the ground beside the girl. He got to his feet and then helped the girl to hers, apologizing profusely. When she spoke back, he noted that she had a Geordie accent and decided that he had made a good choice.

She was of medium height, wearing sandals, a dirndl skirt and white v-necked top. Her hair was fashionably cut short and makeup which had certainly not been professionally applied. He fussed over her and took her into the station café for a cup of tea "to settle both their nerves" after the accident.

Neither of them was badly hurt, but Doyle feigned a slight limp saying that he had twisted his ankle when he tripped over the case. The girl, who gave her name as Marion, said that she was seventeen, on her way to see an aunt who lived in Dunfermline. Doyle didn't believe she was as old as that, and he congratulated himself on his choice. He knew that the last train to Dunfermline left Waverley just after the London train arrived. Unless the girl hired a taxi, which he was sure she could not afford, she was stuck in Edinburgh for the night.

They shared a pot of tea, and Doyle offered to see her to her train. When she realized that she had missed her link she was distraught. "My aunty will be expecting me. What on earth can I do?" Doyle was all charm. "Well, I'm responsible for your predicament, let me pay for a hotel room for you, for the night." He had previously told her that he was a carpenter, and she said," No, I can't have you paying the price of a hotel. There must be something else." He would have been extremely disappointed if she had said anything else.

"I could suggest you come home with me," said Doyle, "but it doesn't seem appropriate, and my wife would probably be very suspicious." Marion then said, "but she'd have nothing to be suspicious about. I'm sure she would believe the two of us when we tell her what happened. Besides, you have the sore ankle to prove we were in an accident."

Doyle congratulated himself at the way his plan was working. "I'll phone her anyway, just to make sure. Then she won't get a shock when we get there." He then went to a phone box and went through the motions of making a phone call while Marion stood outside. He gave her a thumbs-up sign as he came out, then just to create more confidence, he said, "Mary says it will be OK. But she hopes you don't take milk in your coffee or tea.

There's none left in the house. Come on, we'll be in time for the last bus. They climbed the stairs to Princes Street and waited at the bus stop. He explained to Marion that he lived in Dean Village. "It used to be a village, and has kept its name. It's not so far from the West End" The bus was full of people. Although it was nearly midnight, there was still some daylight, and it was clear that people had been enjoying strolls in the balmy evening. Soon after the bus turned off Princes Street to turn towards the northwest they got off, before it crossed the Dean Bridge. As they walked down the brae towards the Water of Leith, Doyle pointed out the old village on the banks of the river. "That's where we are going. We'll be able to see my house soon. They soon arrived at the river's edge, but instead of turning towards the houses Doyle took the girls arm and propelled her towards the riverside path.

Marion started to protest but Doyle had a firm hold on her arm. He threw the case he was carrying into the river then said to the girl. "Don't make any noise. Nobody'll hear you anyway, so it'll do you no good." The girl realized that she had been duped, but tried to act courageously. "You wouldn't. I am only sixteen. You're not going to hurt me, are you?" "Not if you're sensible," said Doyle, not letting go of her arm. When they were underneath the bridge he led her further from the water then pushed her to the ground. "I don't want to hurt you, but if you struggle you will be hurt." He knelt down beside her and pushed up her flimsy top. Reaching behind her, he grabbed at the strap of her bra and pulled it apart. Freed of the restriction, her breasts burst away from the bra revealing a well- developed bust. Doyle became excited at the sight of the young body, and started to pull at her wide skirt. It presented no difficulties to him and was soon revealing a pair of skimpy pants which were torn apart in seconds.

Doyle leaned back to view the girl in her near total nakedness, then started fondling between her thighs. Marion started to whimper, and then she started to struggle, trying to wriggle out from under him. "I told you "he said, "If you struggle you will only get hurt. You are not going anywhere, and you won't be heard here, so do as your told and I might let you go." "You bastard," the girl screamed, "you're not going to let me go. You have planned all this. Now you'll have to kill me, but the police will find you easily. Just do what you want and then go away. I'll give them a false description so they can't get you.

Just leave me, just leave me."

Doyle was amazed at the girl's composure. He had seen many people killed. He had caused the death of several, but this was the first time he had seen anyone so composed, knowing that she was about to die. He himself was calm, no frenzied rage this time, just a feeling of serenity that he was completely in charge. He raped the girl at his ease, and then lay beside her, keeping his arms around her. Marion was amazed that she had not been hurt more viciously. She had known young boys in the past and had enjoyed sex with them. Before being raped she had envisaged being ravaged by a grown adult who would be virtually tearing her apart, but she quickly realized that she had nothing to fear from the size of his organ. If only she could humour him she thought that there was a real chance of getting out of this without too much damage.

She actually started to talk to him in the hope that he would react gently and leave her alone. Despite her youthfulness and inexperience, she had quickly assessed that he was really cunning and twisted up. Each thing that he had done had obviously been carefully planned. Since they had reached the riverside she had realized that he was not married, probably a real mummy's boy who had been deprived of love and kept under his mother's or another adult woman's thumb all his life. But the things he had said had all been so plausible, down to the "wife's" concern that she did not have any milk in the house, that it was only when they had turned onto the riverside path that she had started to feel afraid. Now, with Doyle apparently satisfied after having raped her, she even began to think that that was as far as he was going to go with her.

But Doyle had other ideas. As the girl was talking, he was starting to get all churned up inside. She was no better than any of the prostitutes he had been with, and a lot worse than the two girls he had raped previously. He had risked everything to bring her here, carefully planning every move, yet felt no satisfaction whatsoever. "Shut up," he yelled aat the girl. "Why should I let you go. You are no better than any of the others."

Marion chilled. She took it that he had raped before, and if so, had probably murdered. She had nothing left to do but try and get out of his clutches. She tried to squirm out of his arms but felt the power of his muscles and took another route, kneeing him as hard as she could in the groin. Despite being naked from the waist down, the blow did not hurt too much, and he pushed her away to arms- length and swung a punch at her head. Amazingly she got an arm up to foil his punch, then grabbed at his arm and bit his wrist. She clung on and bit deeply, really clenching her teeth. She now knew she had nothing to lose, but instead of trying to get away from him she went closer to him and dragged her finger nails across the part of his face that was not hidden by his beard. Doyle was taken aback. He was not used to such close fighting, especially from a desperate woman who was fighting for her life.

The pain in his wrist and from his face shocked him. He was so used to dishing out the pain that this was a new experience for him- an experience he did not like. He tried to keep her at arms- length so that he could land a good punch on her, pushing at her shoulder with his left hand, from which blood was pouring from the bite, but without success. She continued to stay close in against him to thwart his punches. As could be expected, however, the girl weakened before he did and he was able to reach her throat with both hands. As she weakened, Doyle experienced the same excitement overtake him as he had experienced with the schoolgirl, so he pushed Marion to the ground again and thrust himself into her once more, experiencing a climax almost immediately, while he listened to the death rattle in her throat.

This time there were no convenient building blocks to cover up the body, so he pulled her back until they were against the abutment of the bridge, as far as possible from the water's edge and covered the body with some of the debris that had been washed down the river when last it had been in spate.

He did not return to the road that he had travelled before. This time he walked along the river bank until he reached Stockbridge. As he walked he was aware of the pain in his wrist where the girl had bitten him. It was only when he neared the end of the path that he realized that the wound had been bleeding a lot and had left the sleeve of his jacket with a large bloodstain. He took off the jacket as he approached the main road, took his wallet from the pocket, ensured he hadn't left anything that might lead the police to him if the jacket was found, then deposited it under a bush

This left him with just a shirt and trousers, but the late June night was still warm, and he would not attract any attention for not wearing a jacket. He bound a hankie around his wrist, crossed Henderson Street at the lights when he was satisfied that no one was about and then travelled eastwards through all the back- doubles until he reached the rear of Gayfield Square Police station, then back to Elm Row where he arrived at his flat having seen no more than half a dozen people on the way, and all of these at some distance. As he entered his flat he felt some kind of gratitude towards Tom Mitchell who had shown him the back- doubles along his route when they had been running together at times.

At home, Doyle showered, put a bandage on his left wrist and applied some healing ointment to the deep scratches around his eyes. He knew that he had been unprepared for the girls fight back. For the first time, apart from the time he himself had been attacked in Aldershot, he was bearing some marks that would be difficult to conceal. He felt fulfilled for the first time since his New Year incident, but had a presentiment that the police would be taking a greater interest in this latest escapade. The following morning he went back to Waverley station to collect the back- pack from the left luggage depot.

It was several days later that the body was found, although the local press had been printing reports of a missing girl from the day after she had disappeared. There had been many appeals for anyone who had seen her either at the station or anywhere else. The description of her, and of what she had been wearing was very accurate. It had been given by the girl's mother in Newcastle. Her aunt in Dunfermline had reported that her niece had not arrived from Edinburgh on the last train as she had expected.

The search for the girl was widespread, but it was only narrowed down to the Dean Village area when a man who had been a passenger on a late-night bus recalled having seen a girl who fitted the description with an older man. They had boarded the bus in Princes Street, near Waverley station, and had dismounted at the stop after Randolph Crescent. The man was described as tall, bearded, too young to be the girl's father and, in the witness's view, too old to be her boyfriend. He was further described as having a limp which showed up when he walked away from the bus with the girl. The witness also recalled having seen the man carrying a suitcase which tallied with the mother's description.

The police investigation for the murderer was concentrated originally in the immediate area around where the body had been found. They assumed that he must have had an intimate knowledge of the area to guide the girl to where she was found. When they made little progress in the locality they extended their enquiries to other parts of the city centre. Armed with a photo-fit picture of the man who had been seen with the murdered girl, a large team of police constables knocked on doors, showed the picture and asked all the men who had any resemblance to the picture where they had been on the night of the murder.

About a week after the murder, Doyle answered a knock at the door. Two uniformed policemen explained what they were seeking, and recognizing some of the characteristics of the alleged murderer, asked some pointed questions. After having read the description in the local press, Doyle had taken to wearing spectacles again. There had been no mention of spectacles so he had adopted them to try and put the police off if he were to be interviewed.

The policemen noted the physical resemblance to the man in the picture, and after hearing Doyle's tale of where he had been that night, made notes that he deserved further questioning. Doyle was therefore asked to attend at Gayfield Square Police station for a line-up of men who fitted the description, along with another dozen men. When Doyle arrived at the police station, the purpose of the line-up was explained. The man who had seen the girl, and her companion, would view all of the men who had been considered as approaching the murderers description. At that point, there was no evidence whatsoever against any of the men in the line-up. The line appeared to be haphazard, a dozen well-built, tall bearded men, three of whom wore spectacles, including Doyle.

The witness passed along the rank of men, making no comment to the detective escorting him. He then left the room and the men were asked to change places, again haphazardly. This process was repeated, but this time the men who wore glasses were asked to remove them. Without his glasses Doyle was very short sighted, and had a cast in his eye, the result of the blow that he had suffered in Aldershot. The appearance of his face changed dramatically as he squinted to try and see better when the witness passed along the line. This time, nine of the men were dismissed from the line-up and the other three were retained for further questioning. Doyle was one of the nine who were dismissed.

When he got back to his flat Doyle heaved a big sigh of relief that he had not been retained, but he assumed that someone among the investigating team would have the thought that any spectacle-wearing man was bound to look entirely different if he wore contact lenses. He resigned himself to a further visit from the police, so worked carefully on an alibi for himself for the night of the murder.

But Doyle had slipped up. In their bid to find any clues in the vicinity of the murder, the search had been gradually extending, and eventually the jacket had been found under the bush where Doyle had hidden it. Doyle's attempt at ensuring that no clues would be left had proved ineffective. He had not taken into consideration any labels that the tailor may have sewn into the suit. In fact, it did not take long for the police to discover that the suit had been sold by John Lewis Partnership to a Miss Margaret Mitchell who lived in Montgomery Street.

CHAPTER 27

Although Tom attended Doyle's classes after the incident with Andrew, he made no effort to re-establish the relationship that they had had previously. What he had learned in Ireland, and had seen at the engagement party, convinced him that Doyle was a very dangerous man. He had read, when filling in on the background to Peter Manuel after his conversation with the Coventry policeman, that many senior legal and psychiatric experts considered Manuel a true psychopath. It was Tom's belief that Doyle had followed in his father's footsteps although he had no evidence of him having killed anyone, apart from the chap in Aldershot. That of course had been deemed to be justifiable homicide in view of the attack that had been madeon Doyle himself.

Tom kept abreast of local news by reading the newspapers, so had known of the rape of a student in Queen's park, and the rape and murder of the West Lothian schoolgirl in the Royal High School grounds. They had meant nothing to Tom, but when he heard of the murder in Dean Village, and read the description of the girl`s companion given by a witness, his mind had immediately jumped to Jim Doyle.

The morning after Doyle had been helping the police with their enquiries, the Scottish morning papers, reporting on the progress being made in the investigation of the murder, contained a reference to a jacket that had been found. When two policemen knocked at the door of Tom Mitchell`s flat enquiring after Margaret Mitchell, he had explained that Miss Mitchell was his sister, that she was the manageress of a department in John Lewis. He had already been seen by the police during their door-to-door enquiries so he was not upset to see them again. However when he was questioned about the jacket, it had not been difficult to convince them that a jacket which fitted a man with a forty-inch chest would not have fitted his own forty-four inches.

Tom had quickly put two and two together and had assumed Doyle`s guilt for the recent Dean Village murder, but how could he avoid having Margaret implicated? He knew that the relationship had cooled a bit after the engagement, but he also knew that Margaret was spending a couple of nights every week with Doyle. He had no reason to believe that their sexual relationship was not continuing, but what would her reaction be if he were to tell her of the latest situation?

It had been difficult to bring up the subject of Doyle with Margaret after the engagement incident. She had resented what Tom had told her, or his somewhat jaundiced personal view of the incident, and frequently made caustic comments about how Doyle was continuing to pay while Andrew was off work. When she had made the suggestion about coming to terms, she did not think it would last more than a few weeks. Now, after more than two and a half months, the caustic comments were becoming bitter recriminations. In the circumstances Tom had to keep his suspicions to himself.

After the police had departed, Tom called Doyle and suggested that they meet in the evening for a run. At first Doyle was reluctant, but when Tom insisted they agreed to meet at the Holyrood entrance to Queen's Park.

It had been just the previous night that Tom had turned up at a class, to be told by one of the policemen in the class, one who had been at the engagement party, that Doyle was at the police station that night, being interrogated about the murder. This had set Tom's mind whirling. The rest of the people in the class had gone home but Tom stayed at the entrance to the gym to try and see Doyle when he returned. It was late when Doyle arrived wearing his glasses and looking quite harassed.

Doyle had been surprised to see Tom, who said, in a joking manner, "they must have believed your story if they didn't keep you in?" Doyle looked angry and muttered something about just being asked back to help them with their inquiries, seemingly implying that someone else was under suspicion and he was just having to confirm some previous statement he had made. When they met at the Holyrood gate there was a distinctly chilly air between them. There was some small talk, but it was about quarter of an hour before Tom summoned the courage to ask, "Well, are you going to tell me what is happening. I don't suppose you've said anything to Margaret about seeing the police. Are you going to tell me anything about it?"

"There's not a lot to tell", said Doyle. "You probably read about the murder in Dean Village, and read the description of the man who is supposed to have done it. Like dozens of others, I fitted the description. They came to my door, just like they must have come to yours. That night I`d gone out running on my own and I had no way of proving it, so I was added to their list. A dozen of us had to go for a line-up in front of the witness who gave the description. We each had to see a detective who was asking a lot of questions. Nobody was charged, and nobody was detained."

"And where did you go running?" asked Tom.

"Look, I`ve no need to answer any of your questions, so don`t start in on me. I had enough of you when I was in hospital that time." Doyle was angry and was holding nothing back. "You fucking near accused me of murdering that English bastard. You were wrong then, and you`re fucking wrong now if you think I murdered that girl."

Tom sensed that Doyle was feeling a lot of tension, so he kept on at him. "I was not wrong. You did kill the chap, and I still maintain that you egged him on to set up the chance to kill him. If you hadn`t had the intention, you could`ve just disabled him. You are a fucking black belt man. How could you not have held back?"

Doyle was furious. "You are just like the others."

"What others? What the fuck are you talking about?"

"Your fucking mates in the Military Police. That time in Londonderry. They wouldn`t believe what I was saying either. They accused me of firing the first shot that day, and then they charged me for fighting with the ones who did pull the trigger. You are all the fucking same. The civil police are no different.

You hear a Glasgow accent and assume right away that he must have been the one. Well, they were wrong, and you`re wrong as well."

"They were never proved wrong in Londonderry, just like you were never proved innocent. Your Commanding Officer got you off because he couldn't face having the regiment go through the courts for what you did. That enquiry is still going on, and it will do for years. Then it will all be swept under the carpet, just like the case in Aldershot. You've been the lucky bastard both times. You should have been in prison for both of these."

Doyle looked as if he would blow a fuse, but he seemed to get a grip of himself and just walked along for a few minutes without speaking again. By this time they had walked along the lower road of the park and had turned up toward Dunsapie loch. As they reached that point Tom suggested that instead of staying on the road they should climb up Arthur's seat and then descend along the top of Salisbury Crags down to the Holyrood entrance again. Doyle agreed to this. There was plenty of daylight left. The route would be more strenuous than the road, but it would cut a good mile off the distance.

The climb to the top of Arthurs Seat from this direction was not difficult. Women and children could manage it with ease. Tom and Doyle maintained an even pace until about fifty feet from the top. Walking side by side, Tom tried to involve Doyle inmore conversation. "Do you believe in coincidence?" he asked. Doyle seemed to be taken by surprise by this question. "Why the hell do you ask that."

"You mentioned that girl who was murdered." said Tom. "There was another girl raped and murdered at New Year, and last autumn there was a girl raped here in Queens Park."

"Where the hell is the coincidence in that? Girls get raped and murdered all the time. What the fuck are you talking about?" Doyle sounded genuinely puzzled, no note of anger or dismay in his voice.

Tom knew he was on dangerous ground, but kept going. "When I read about the first rape, it just registered in my mind that the place was one that I knew well. You and I have run round that way many times. The murder at the New Year was not so far from here, again on a route that I showed you when we ran together. And now this latest one, a wee bit further away, but on another circuit that I showed you. That's the coincidence." "Christ, you talk a lot of shit. How many people in Edinburgh know all the places you are talking about? There must be thousands. Are you implying that I committed these rapes and murders?"

"I'm just saying that to me it doesn't seem like a coincidence. I had to train just like a policeman and I can't stop myself from linking different things, just like these rapes, then the fact I know about some of your history."

"What the fuck do you know about me? That I got involved in a brawl where someone died, that the army wanted me out because I bashed some stupid paras around. That's not much of a basis for building some kind of story round me, is it?"

Tom felt pleased that at last he could get things out in the open, so he determined to plough on. He had spent the whole day preparing for just such a confrontation. He had been going over all the things he had learned, and although he had no proof of any of them, he felt inside himself that he was very close to the truth.

They did not climb the final fifty feet to the summit, but skirted round to where the more even ground stopped at the edge of the near vertical face of Salisbury Crags. The path was fairly level here, with no greenery apart from the grass, so they faced a long straight stretch that would bring them to a point above Holyrood Palace where they could leave the park. Walking here was simple, no need to watch their footing, so it was possible to concentrate on the conversation.

"No. If that was all, I`d be on weak ground. But I know about the wee boy that was pushed under the tractor. There was the schoolboy you gave a hammering to on the football pitch, and the rugby player you put in hospital. There was even the two Karate men that you sorted out. I`ve done my homework. I think you`re sick, and quite capable of anything."

Doyle was clearly taken aback by these revelations, but wouldn`t give in without a fight. `What can you know about it? I just had a mother to look after me. I never knew my father, and my mother wouldn`t even talk about him. She wouldn`t let me play with other children and she banned me from even talking to girls. That kind of thing gets you a bit screwed up. The teachers wanted me to have a psychiatric check because of my aggression, but my mother wouldn`t have it. I think she was scared to find out something that would have revealed her own past so nothing was done. I`ve often regretted that. Do you think it`s nice to know that you`re capable of hurting people?" Strangely, Doyle was now speaking quite rationally, saying more than Tom had ever heard from him in all the time he had known him.

Tom`s reaction was to wonder whether he should in fact be feeling sorry for Doyle, but kept on in an attempt to get the truth from him." Maybe it was just to protect you that she didn`t tell you the truth. Maybe she just loved you too much." "Loved me too much? We hated each other! If she loved me too much why did she commit suicide?"

"Because she found out the truth about your father. It was too much for her."

Doyle looked blankly at Tom. "What the fuck are you talking about? What could she have found out that she hadn`t known before?"

Tom realised that what he said next would be like opening Pandora`s box, but he kept on. If it wasn`t aired now it never would be. He suggested that they should sit down and talk. Doyle seemed to sense that Tom had something serious to say so promptly sat down, some few yards from the edge of Salisbury Crags. Tom actually felt some sympathy for Doyle. It was hardly his fault that his father had been a rapist and murderer.

"Do you remember the date on which your mother died?" asked Tom.

"Not exactly", said Doyle, "but what has that got to do with anything?"

"Well, it was the 11th of July 1958. On the same day, a murderer who had been found guilty of seven murders and various rapes and assaults, was hung in Barlinnie Prison."

"For Christ`s sake, get on with it. What does all this mean?"

"The man that made your mother pregnant wasn`t called Doyle. She`d been raped, and had never known the man`s name until the day she died, and then only because the man`s picture was in the paper that day. You had a big argument with her. She was upset at that and seeing that man`s face pushed her over the edge. I believe that man, Peter Manuel, was your father." "Fucking rubbish! How could anyone know all this?" "The last thing your mother did before she took those pills that killed her was to write to her grandfather and enclose a copy of the paper that showed Manuel`s picture. The poor woman had been lying to you for years, to protect you from knowing that your father was a rapist, and all you did was show her that you were cast in the same mould. That poor woman had been raped, had a baby at sixteen and been cast out of her family, but loved and protected you all these years and you hated her!" "I don`t believe any of this" said Doyle, "But what the fuck has it got to do with you?"

Tom soon explained. "I knew you were vicious from that first time we met. You had no need to kill that young English chap. You`d been trained not to harm your opponents, but you went ahead. I don`t doubt there have been others, especially those two young girls that were murdered recently in Edinburgh, but it`s all about to end. The police know that it was you. By the time you get home they`ll be waiting for you. You finally made a mistake. The police came to see me this morning, meaning to arrest me for that murder in Dean Village. But they came for the wrong man."

This caught Doyle`s attention. "You! Why would you be under suspicion?"

"Because you threw away the blood-stained jacket you were wearing when you raped and murdered that young girl. Margaret bought that suit for you from her shop, and they were able to trace it back to her. The police thought that it was mine, but accepted that it was too small for me. You`ll be the next one on their list."

Doyle took Tom`s statement very calmly. "I thought that was the best planned one that I`d ever done. But I had a funny feeling about it. It all worked so well, too."

"So are you admitting that there have been others?" asked Tom.

"What use is there in not admitting it to you?" asked Doyle. "You are not going to tell anyone else. How the hell did you learn all this anyway?"

Tom decided that it was now the time to reveal the things he had learned. They continued to sit on the grass, and continued their conversation, now in calm tones and both speaking very rationally. Tom told of the things he had discovered, and how he had discovered them. Doyle was obviously impressed at the way Tom had gathered his information. He listened carefully, without interruption.

When Tom had finished Doyle expressed his amazement at what he had learned. But when Tom then asked how Doyle had started the killing he took up the story-tellers role. He was calm and coherent, showing no sign of holding back.

"When my mother died I was very angry. I couldn't understand why she couldn't tell me about my father. I see why now, but that day we had a big argument. We were shouting at each other. I lost my head and threatened to hit her. She told me to go ahead. She called me a monster, just like my father. I didn't know what she meant, but I ran away. The next time I saw her she was dead. They said she died of a drug overdose. I knew she did it because of our fight."

"I lived with Gran Wilsher after that. She spoiled me. Even more than my mother did. Got me a job at the factory her husband used to own. She made plans for me to marry, live with her and have a family, but I didn't want any of that. One day I told her that I was going to join the army. She went mad. We had a big argument. She told me that she would cancel her will. She said she had left me the house.

I threatened her with a good hammering, and she said the same thing my mother had said. 'Yes, you would, you're a monster just like your father was." "I got so angry with her that I planned how to get rid of her. It worked very well. I made it look like an accident, and the police accepted it."

"Christ, you killed your own grandmother?" burst in Tom.

"No, she was not my real grandmother".

"And she's not the only one you have killed" asked Tom. "Now you have two young girls on your conscience as well."

"Yes. You are right. But you'll never be able to tell anyone about it. You are the next one to go. Over the edge of the crags." Saying this, he made a grab at Tom. But Tom had seen what was coming and sprang away from Doyle before he could be grasped. Tom had half expected something like this to happen, had in fact planned that it should happen, so he had put a flick- knife in his pocket before he left home. As the two men stood several feet apart, looking at each other, Tom pulled the knife from his pocket.

Doyle laughed, "You don't think you'll save yourself with that small thing, do you? Are you forgetting I learned all about unarmed combat and Karate. Just make up your mind you're going over the edge. This will be better than any of the killings or rapes. None of the others put up much of a fight. I'll tell Margaret and the police that we were just scrapping and you fell over the edge."

With that Doyle made a rush at Tom, but Tom managed to evade the first charge. By keeping the five inch blade held out he effectively prevented Doyle from using any close fighting tactics so for several minutes the two kept circling each other, seeking an opening. Tom knew that if he let

Doyle close in on him, he could kiss his chances of survival goodbye. But Tom had learned something at Karate. For weeks he had watched Doyle perfect a high kicking action at his opponents head or shoulder. When done properly all the weight was balanced on the one foot while the other foot kicked out to disable the opponent.

Tom himself had thought of a move to counteract this. It was chancy, but he could think of no other way to get the upper hand.

When Doyle pressed forward to get into range to do his flying kick, instead of retreating Tom held his ground. As Doyle started his movement Tom ducked down and dived under the flailing leg. While Doyle was still rooted on his one leg, Tom brought the knife upwards with a vicious thrust into Doyle`s groin. Doyle let out a scream and fell back to the ground with the handle of the knife protruding from his trousers like a wooden penis

Tom knew that the blow in itself wasn`t fatal. He couldn`t afford to give Doyle a second chance to attack him so he took hold of one of his legs and pulled him to the edge of the crags. Doyle looked Tom straight in the eye and said his last words "I fucking knew you were going to cause me trouble the minute you walked into my gym. Tom applied the last bit of pressure that took Doyle over the edge. Tom peered over the edge as the body hurtled downwards, bouncing against the rock face until it reached the loose shale that formed a slope at the base of the precipice. He had no regrets. It was always going to be a fight to the death once Tom had started the conversation. Both of them had known it. Tom`s plan had turned out more successful than Doyle`s.

CHAPTER 28

As night drew in on the hill, Tom made his way down. Everything had gone to plan so far, but he now faced the hardest part, telling his sister about Doyle Margaret looked very upset when he arrived home, and she was first to speak. "I've been trying to get Jim for ages. I wanted to to talk to him about that suit I bought for him. When I got home there were a couple of police here. They were asking questions about a jacket. They wouldn't say why they were interested in the jacket."

"I've no idea where he is," said Tom, "He didn't turn up for the class last night but I saw him afterwards. He had been asked to take part in an identity parade along with a lot of others at Gayfield Square Police station. "The police came here this morning. They were asking about the jacket that was found. It was traced back to you and they thought it must be mine. They left when they realised that a 40" chest jacket was never meant for a person my size."

Margaret looked puzzled. "But what was so important about a jacket? Jim had told me that he lost it, and his wallet, in a fight." "Well, maybe he did. But the police found it hidden under a bush not far from where that girl was murdered in the Dean Village. They are apparently linking it to the murder. It had bloodstains on the sleeve."

Margaret sounded indignant, but Tom could detect a hint of resignation in her voice. He could sense that this clever sister had already started to put two and two together when she had seen the police.

"Didn't you know that he missed last night's class because he was being questioned by the police for the second time, in connection with that murder. The first time was when the police were carrying out door to door checks. They came here. I had to answer their questions. They must have thought it was worthwhile seeing Doyle again.

"God", said Margaret, "I didn't know anything about that. But he doesn't tell me very much at any time. I told you before that he had changed a lot, but recently he has gone back to how he used to be, maybe even more reticent. Since that night at the engagement party I have gone off him a bit. I thought he had changed but he hadn't really. I haven't seen him in over a week. We have been so busy at work with sales on, and last weekend I was watching Bob Fernie playing in a golf tournament at Muirfield and stayed with his family. You remember Bob, he was at the engagement party and you've met him several times. "It is strange, that last time I saw Jim, I had gone round to his flat. You know I've got a key. I went round about ten o'clock. He was not there when I arrived, but I watched something on television and fell asleep on his settee. It was very late when he got home. He was quite dishevelled. He had a bandage on his wrist and a scratch on his face. He told me that he had got caught up in a fight at the foot of Leith Walk. Two chaps apparently set upon him, one of them with a knife. They took his jacket and his wallet. He said he left them in a worse state than he was in.

"Strangely enough, he seemed a bit different. In bed he was very loving and was a lot more enthusiastic about having sex than he usually is. But next morning he was back to his usual moody nature. Really, I have gone off him a bit. I think I made a mistake. He would be too difficult to live with. I`d be far better off with Bob. Life would be a lot easier. If the police can`t find him, maybe he has done a bunk. I won`t cry over it."

Tom could see that, even as she spoke, she was putting two and two together and had already accepted that her fiancé had been involved with the murder of the girl under the Dean Bridge. He did not try to console her or to make a case for Doyle`s innocence.

After having talked with his sister, Jim began to consider his own situation. He had walked away from Queen`s park without giving any thought to what would happen when Doyle`s body was discovered, but now he began to fear that the police would have no difficulty in associating him with Doyle, and his fingerprints would be found on theknife.

He gradually prepared a plan in his mind, and, long after midnight, when he was convinced that Margaret was asleep, he let himself out of the house, armed with a strong torch and a pair of leather gardening gloves.

He met no one on the short walk back to Queens Park. Entering the park from the road that provided access to the breweries close to Holyrood Palace, he started to climb the path known as the Radical Road which followed fairly close to the vertical face of the crags.

He could remember roughly just where he had pushed Doyle over the edge so did not have to start scrambling over the scree which lay between the face and the path until he was close to where he expected to find the body. When he left the path it became very rough underfoot. He had to use his torch to avoid falling. The torch had a shield on it which restricted the beam and as he was some way from the road he felt sure that he was not visible to anyone.

Staying close to the vertical face he soon came upon Doyle's body. The major part of his plan was to remove the knife from the body so that it could not be traced to him, and the second part was to cover the body as well as he could so that it would be some time before it was discovered. The body was some yards from the near vertical face of the rock. It seemed clear that in falling it had hit a projection on the face of the rock and had been thrown outwards.

Tom was shocked at the injuries to the body, but gritted his teeth, removed the knife and carefully wiped it clean with his handkerchief. He then pulled the body, by the feet, as close to the vertical face as possible, then, with his hands encased in the leather gloves he had brought, created a shallow grave in the loose scree, covered the body with loose shale, topping it off with loose rocks as large as he could handle.

The whole operation took him more than three hours and as he walked home he hoped that he had done sufficient to delay the discovery of the body and to hide any evidence that wouldpoint to himself. Despite the physical effort that he had gone through, Tom did not sleep well when at last he climbed into bed.

The police called on Margaret again at her office the following morning and questioned her about where they might find Doyle.

She was able to tell them truthfully that she had not seen Doyle the previous day. After the police had visited her at er office she had tried to contact him by phone on several occasions without success. The detective sergeant, Alan Spence, and the plain clothed woman constable who accompanied him would not reveal why they wanted to talk to Doyle, but asked Margaret to contact them immediately if he got in touch with her.

The detectives realised that Doyle had probably accepted that the police had already collected sufficient evidence to establish his guilt for the murder in Dean Village but now they started devoting a lot of time collecting any other evidence that might implicate him in any other crimes and to find out where he was now. A major police enquiry was set up, the press and other media were notified and soon the description of Jim Doyle was distributed and appeals for any viewings of him were distributed throughout Britain.

The police concentrated on establishing a profile of this ex- paratrooper who had set up a karate club in the centre of Edinburgh. As information was received from his schools, his karate coach, the military authorities, his army colleagues and the priest who had taken him under his wing, the police started to wonder how on earth such a time-bomb could have eluded their notice for so long?

Much of the evidence that was revealed came from the press. Reporters picked up on many incidents that Doyle had been involved in, but none of them came close to the story that had died with the death of Mary, his mother, and the surrogate grandmother who had died in a domestic accident and had left her entire fortune to him.

A nationwide search for Doyle revealed no clues whatsoever to Doyle's whereabouts. There were no clues from airports, railway or bus stations, or ferries. The police had gone through his flat with a fine tooth comb, but nothing incriminating had been found. His passport was found in a bureau, as were his bank statements for the past year.

As there were no mortgage payments included on the statements, it was assumed that he owned the property in Elm Row. That, and the cash balance that had remained fairly constant, revealed that Doyle was quite comfortably rich. From the documents in the bureau they learned the name of the Edinburgh solicitor who had represented him in the purchase of the property and they quickly contacted him to find out whether there was a will, or any indication of relatives who could be contacted. Nothing came to light on where he might have gone and his disappearance soon drew less and less attention from the press.

The police, however, continued their investigations into the rape of the student in Queen's Park, the death of the young girl whose body had been found in Royal High School grounds, and the one who had been found under the Dean Bridge. They followed up on the jacket that had been found and had concluded that the ownership had been proved and that Doyle's disappearance so soon after having been interviewed for the second time pointed to his guilt in at least the latest of the crimes.

There had been no response from the public regarding his movements during that last day before his disappearance, but in retrospect the police accepted that Doyle had had the facility to change his looks completely simply by wearing heavy glasses instead of contact lenses and by saving off the beard that he had worn for some time. Mugshots of him in the various possibilities were distributed throughout Britain but there was little response from the public, and those responses that the police had were soon proved to be misleading.

CHAPTER 29

Soon after Doyle's disappearance Margaret announced to her friends that she would not be seeing any more of Doyle, and in fact had accepted Bob Fernie's proposal of marriage. This was not strictly true for Margaret had realized, around the same time as the disappearance, that she was some days late with her monthly period, and having already accepted that she would not be continuing her relationship with Doyle had initiated the conversation about marriage with Bob.

Margaret's friends, who had not thought the match very fitting, were delighted at her decision to marry Bob, and his friends were quick to congratulate Bob on finally winning the woman that they had all foreseen as the eventual Mrs Fernie. Those friends main concern was that they would see less of Bob on the golf course where he was the best of their group, playing off a handicap of six. Bob had been educated at Loretto School in Musselburgh. Although he was born and brought up close to Musselburgh he had been a boarder at Loretto during his entire school life.

He had started playing golf at a very early age and had never been away from it. At one time he had excelled, getting down to scratch and representing Scotland as an amateur, but an injury to his arm when playing rugby at age 25 had prevented him from maintaining his low handicap, but still let him play seriously good golf.

His family were disappointed that Bob and Margaret did not have a big church wedding, but they hosted a large reception for the couple at Royal Musselburgh Golf Club, where all Bob's family were members. Margaret felt quite at home in the lush surroundings and with the rather exalted company, but Tom felt a bit out of place.

His life had not prepared him for the company of bankers, industrialists, golfers and university trained people. In the speech that he made he expressed his delight that the couple had finally got together after having known each other for so long, while wondering within himself how he would have felt if the marriage between Margaret and Doyle had gone ahead.

After a brief honeymoon in the South of France Margaret and Bob moved into a three bedroom detached house about halfway between their respective homes. Their work places were fairly close to each other so they travelled in to the centre of Edinburgh together in Bob's Rover. Margaret was quick to point out to Bob that she would be requiring a car for herself when the baby came along.

The baby, a healthy, bawling girl arrived at the due time and as with all new parents life immediately became totally different. They had already agreed that Margaret should not give up her job but should take six months leave after the birth. They had also discussed their ambitions to have a larger house, with some land around it which would necessitate a mortgage so the plan was to build up as large a deposit as possible towards the new house, and have another child within three to four years.

A daughter, whom they named Teresa duly arrived at the forecast time in Spring 1979. She looked like a miniature of her mother, which relieved Margaret's fears that the baby would turn out to look like Doyle. She also feared that the baby might inherit his vicious streak. She would not know how to cope with the situation if her fears came true, but was consoled by the thought that the warmth and safety of loving parents would create a lot more loving environment for the child than Doyle had ever known.

Margaret and Bob quickly settled into married life and parentage. Teresa showed no signs of being anything other than a normal child. She was robust, consumed her feeds well and did not cause many sleepless nights for her parents. As she approached the age of six months Margaret and Bob made plans for Teresa to join a day-nursery which took children from that age and kept them until they reached school age.

Handing over her daughter to strangers did not appeal to Margaret, but she was reluctant to discard the executive role that she had with John Lewis and had to grit her teeth and face up to seeing her daughter for only an hour each morning and evening on weekdays. Until Teresa started at nursery, Bob had continued to enjoy his game of golf each Saturday and Sunday morning at his local golf club, Royal Musselburgh, but the new arrangement meant that he had to help Margaret with household, shopping and gardening chores that piled up when Margaret went back to work. Arguments became quite frequent between Bob and Margaret, mainly over the amount of attention Teresa should be given during weekends, and as happens often, the child started to become quite spoiled, getting endless attention from one parent or the other during the entire weekend. Each little cry resulted in her being picked up and fondled.

It became quite clear to Bob's parents, and to Tom Mitchell, all frequent visitors at weekends, that there was some conflict occurring between Bob and Margaret over who could command the child's attention. None of the visitors spoke to the parents about this, despite all cringing when they witnessed the frequent incidents between them. Teresa wanted for nothing. Between her grandparents, her parents and her uncle- and friends of her parents- she was the possessor of a huge trunk of toys that she had no use for, and only a few of which she was interested in. Many of the toys came from guests at Teresa's christening party which took place when she was six months old. It was evident to Tom at the party that the friends of Bob and Margaret were all from wealthy backgrounds. No expense seemed to have been spared in selecting gifts that Tom considered away beyond what should be given to young children. The same thing happened again at Teresa's first Christmas and on her first birthday. Tom felt that lavishing so much on a young child would lead to the child being spoiled, and in fact he said as much to his sister, but she pooh-poohed the idea.

Tom and Mary, and her son David, were by now accepted by Bob and Margaret as part of their family and they were frequent visitors to the Fernie household. David was only a year and a half older than Teresa and he took a great interest in her- and her toys. Before she could walk David would have free access to all the toys in the trunk, and in the garage, for some of the toys were too big to keep indoors, and he loved to play on her bike, kick the balls and play with the huge Lego set that she had.

However, soon after she turned a year old, Teresa started to walk and took to following David around when he visited. Suddenly she became very proprietary about her toys, even those that she had shown no interest in previously and whenever David picked something out of the trunk, mounted her bike, played with the balls or opened her books she would throw a tantrum until he returned them to her. Tom and Mary could see what was happening, and to try and avoid these tantrums, they would bring a book with them which would keep David occupied, but which would not be of interest to Teresa. This ploy worked well and for a long time there was no serious conflict between the two children but of course it was impossible to ensure that there were no serious incidents- at least at home.

It was a different matter at the nursery that Teresa attended. The carers there were frequently near demented with her antics at times. Only toys that the school provided were made available to the children within their play areas. The carers tried to encourage the toddlers to share them all and normally they were quite successful, but when Teresa was introduced to new classes, year by year, and to new toys, books and educational games she went through the same process of trying to lay claim to everything as her own.

Promotion at work meant Bob could afford to employ a part time housekeeper, which freed him from the chores that Margaret kept finding for him, and which prevented him from playing golf as often as he would like to. The changed circumstances set Margaret thinking about having the larger house that they planned on and to have a second child. When Teresa passed her third birthday Margaret started to push her husband to support her plans. She wanted the bigger house, with extra bedrooms, larger garden and a double garage. By this time Bob had upgraded his car to a Porsche and it was Margaret who was driving a Rover. She constantly complained that it was not right for her car to stand outside at nights while Bob`s was in the garage. To Margaret, a double garage was a necessity. She had set her sights on an older detached house fairly close to her own which belonged to a senior colleagues of Bob`s. When this colleague was promoted within the bank and had to move south Bob made a deal with him to buy his house. The purchase went through very smoothly and the family moved into the new house halfway through Teresa`s fourth year.

Things went very well for the Fernies but Margaret was concerned that Teresa would become very spoilt, so suggested to Bob that they should have another child. Bob agreed. His income could certainly support the lifestyle that they had established, even if Margaret were to leave her job for a while. She stopped using the pills that she had been using since Teresa`s birth, and kept hoping that she would conceive again before she would be too old to cope with the situation.

Unfortunately, their efforts still had not been successful after a year. Of his own accord, Bob visited a clinic to be tested for his ability to become a father and was shocked to hear that he was infertile. For a few months he kept this to himself but an incident that would wreck their comfort was not far away.

By this time David had started at primary school but still accompanied Tom and Mary on odd weekends to visit the Fernie family. On these visits David would condescend to play with Teresa actually sharing her bike and the more mature toys that she had accumulated, but Teresa still insisted on exerting her own will over what he could play with. On one such visit to the new house, when Teresa was about four and a half years old, after a heavy lunch on a wet Sunday afternoon, David and Teresa were sent out to play in the garage while the adults sat around to let the effects of the food and wine wear off.

In the garage, Bob had taken his golf clubs out of the car and stood them against the wall so that he could clean them off after lunch. David spotted the clubs and went towards the bag. He lifted out the putter and went through the procedure he had seen Bob doing on several occasions, swinging the club wildly. Teresa at first went for her bike, to get there before David, but when she saw him swinging the club, she made to grab it. The children tugged and pulled at the club, David with his hand on the head and Teresa's hands on the grip. Teresa was screaming at the top of her voice that the club was hers and David, with a very ill grace, conceded it to her. In a tantrum, Teresa swung the club at David. It was a wild swing, but David ducked straight into it and the putter head hit him in the left eye. He let out a scream and Teresa ran into the house.

Tom led the charge into the garage where they found David on the floor, hand clutched over his eye. He turned round to talk to Margaret who was close behind him holding Teresa's hand. Tom caught the young girl's eye, and a shudder went through him. She had a nasty look of satisfaction, which immediately reminded him of the look on Jim Doyle's face when he badly injured the young guest at Margaret's engagement party. He was also reminded of the story that Doyle's great grandfather had told him about the child Doyle pushing another young boy under a tractor.

It was clear that the injury was serious and Bob immediately called for an ambulance. Mary was in hysterics and the men tried to calm her down while they waited for the ambulance to arrive, but Margaret was demanding of Teresa just what had happened.

All Teresa could say was that they had been playing and David got in the way.

Mary went off in the ambulance with David while Tom followed them in his car. He had seen Teresa in her tantrums on many occasions, especially when she had fought over toys with David, and having seen the state she was in when she has run into the house, he suspected it was the same thing, except this time no toys had been involved, but a potential dangerous weapon. For years he had pushed into the back of his mind the possibility that Teresa was the daughter of Jim Doyle. Had he not succeeded in finishing off the Manuel legacy when he pushed Doyle over that cliff?

At the hospital, an eye specialist was quickly contacted and within two hours from when the incident happened, Mary and Tom learned that the damage to David's left eye was irreparable. The end of the putter had apparently struck exactly on the pupil and the blow had been of sufficient force to explode the soft substance, without any damage to the bone socket. The couple were devastated.

David's injury was treated and a dressing applied to his eye. He had to stay in hospital for several days under the close supervision of the eye specialist. When he left hospital, physically well apart from the eye injury, he was wearing an eye patch over the now empty eye socket.

When Tom returned to Margaret's home on his own, anxious to establish just what had happened, he had to tell Teresa's parents that David had lost his eye. He found Margaret in tears over the situation. She had come to love David, whom she had known from his birth, having lived in the same tenement building and considered his mother her best friend. To learn that he had lost an eye and through something her daughter had done, devastated her.

She had tried to get Teresa to tell her just what happened, but apart from repeatedly hearing "We were just fighting for the putter and David got hurt in the face". In the waiting room in the hospital David's explanation had been "She got the putter from me and then swung it at me like she has seen her daddy doing it in the garden. I slipped and fell forward and the thing hit me in the eye."

Bob was very upset, saying he was sorry that he had left his clubs where the children could get at them. Normally he did not take the clubs out of his car, but all his equipment had got wet with the rain during his round and he had left them out to remind him that everything needed to be wiped clean. The putter was the only club that he had ever let Teresa play with while he messed about with his clubs in the back garden, and she had obviously felt that she had a claim towards the putter. He had shown her how to putt but she had also seen him swinging the other clubs to hit a practice ball so he presumed that she had been trying to swing the putter like an ordinary stroke and David had been in the way.

Teresa herself confirmed that she had tried to swing the putter like a golf club and David slipped towards her as she swung. She told Tom she was sorry that David was hurt, but she did not appear to be very upset.

Tom heard all of their stories. He was reluctant to believe that Teresa might have swung the club deliberately meaning to hit David, but there was no way it could ever be proved. Could a child under four years old have that kind of intent? Tom wondered about it and determined to read up about when vicious traits develop in children who were fathered by a known psychopath. He was unable to get out of his mind the thoughts that he had had in the hospital. Was Teresa in fact the child of Jim Doyle, and had she inherited the genes that would drive her to doing such a thing deliberately?

If Margaret had any thoughts like Tom's she certainly wasn't talking about them. Since her marriage to Bob she had occasionally felt a bit guilty that she may have been pregnant by Doyle when she got together again with Bob, but her guilty feelings did not incorporate the possibility that her daughter might inherit any of the Doyle genes that had driven him to rape and murder. But then, Tom had never revealed to her the full extent of what he had found out about Doyle, and about the father, Peter Manuel.

When Teresa was in bed that night, Margaret said to Bob" I wish we had thought earlier about having another child. I think that Teresa would be less inclined to try and keep everything to herself. That accident would never have happened if she could have learned to share things with others. Do you think we will ever have another?"

Bob realized that he would have to reveal what he had been so silent about for the past few months. "We are never going to have any more children. In fact, I now know for sure that Teresa is not my daughter. I am infertile, I'll never father a child" Margaret was shocked. Although she had told Bob about her pregnancy before their wedding, the subject had never come up again. They both loved each other very much. Their lives had been as close to married bliss as either of them could have desired, without any mention of Doyle having come up between them. Now it seemed that they were to be split. After more than five years tiptoeing past the subject to avoid rancour between them, it seemed that a major row was now inevitable. However, Bob was the first to attempt at damping any animosity. "I am not going to make an issue out of this. I accepted the situation when we married. We have had a good life. Occasionally I have thought that we are both so alike in temperament that Teresa could not possibly have been ours, but I was not going to let that get between us. I am still determined that we will not be affected by this. But we can no longer ignore the subject. We will need to keep a close eye on our daughter." Margaret was surprised, and pleased, that he had spoken of "our daughter". "Oh, Bob, I thought that our life was going to be so straightforward, but I suppose this was always going to happen. Do you really mean it? Can we continue as we have done up to now?"

When she was alone, Margaret thought about Teresa's father, the man who had disappeared following the murder of a young girl, and the questions that had been asked about other murders and rapes in Edinburgh around the same time. She tried to put two and two together and came to the conclusion that her daughter had possibly inherited the genes of a psychopath. What did the future hold for them?

AUTHOR`S NOTE

I was living in Edinburgh in 1958, at the time of Peter Manuel`s trial. I recall having said to my wife "I hope he has not left any children."

The thought stayed with me for many years and when I took a course in Creative Writing at York University at the start of the 21st century I decided to create a novel centred on the subject. My book was originally published under the title "The Manuel Legacy" in 2007. but it received little response. After further research recently, I came upon the following item, while browsing through Google, which led to me completing this rewrite.

John Bathgate

Peter Manuel *(March 1, 1927 – July 11, 1958) was a U.S.-born <u>serial killer </u>who is considered one of the most psychopathic killers in British criminal history. He was the second last person to be hanged in Barlinnie Prison and the third last to be hanged in Scotland.*

Early life

Born in New York to Scottish parents, Manuel and his family moved to Coventry, England in 1932. Considered a juvenile delinquent throughout childhood, Manuel's first jail term was at age 16 for sexual assault. He served further sentences for rape before moving to Glasgow, Scotland in 1953 to join his family, who had moved there. It was in Glasgow that he began his killing spree.

Murders

He was questioned in 1956 for the <u>murder</u> of 17-year-old Anna Knielands, who had been attacked with a length of iron and whose body was discovered on East Kilbride golf course. He was released without charge, but would later confess to the murder in 1958. On September 17, 1956, the bodies of 45-year- old Marion Watt, her 16-year-old daughter Vivienne, and Marion's sister Margaret were found dead at the Watts' home in Burnside, Glasgow. They had all been shot at close range. The police officer in charge suspected Manuel, who had been out on bail for a burglary at a local colliery. Manuel was questioned again to no avail and two weeks later was jailed for 18 months for the colliery burglary.

On his release, Manuel visited Newcastle Upon Tyne in early December 1957, where he shot and killed taxi driver Sydney Dunn. Returning to Glasgow, Manuel's random killings continued, and a real sense of fear gripped the city. On December 27, 1957, 17-year-old Isabelle Cooke left home to go to a dance but never returned. Her body was later found buried in a field. On January 1, 1958, Manuel gunned down

45-year-old Peter Smart, his wife Doris, and their 10-year-old son Michael in Uddingston. After the killing, he returned to the house frequently to rest up, help himself to food, and drive around in the family's car. He fed the murdered family's cat whenever he made one of his visits.

Trial

Twelve days later, Manuel was arrested when the new bank notes he took from the Smarts' home aroused the suspicion of a local bartender. The police traced the notes to Peter Smart and arrested Manuel, who was charged with seven murders. Having been brought to trial several times during his adulthood, he was a master at skilfully providing his own defense in court and escaped conviction more than once. He shifted blame from himself so skilfully that the innocent widower of one of his first victims was temporarily jailed on suspicion of having committed Manuel's crime. At his final trial at Glasgow High Court, Manuel again conducted his own defence but was unable to convince the judge of his insanity plea. He was found guilty in May 1958 of seven murders, although many connected with the case believe he killed up to 15 people. He was hanged at Barlinnie prison, Glasgow on July 11, 1958. His last words were, "Turn up the radio and I'll go quietly."

This book has not yet been published. I would be grateful for any comments you may like to give. jebswrite@gmail.com

John Bathgate
February 2017

Printed in the United States
By Bookmasters